# FLESH AND IRON

## DELTA SQUAD BOOK 5

### JESSE WILSON

Copyright © 2024 by Jesse Wilson

Layout design and Copyright © 2024 by Next Chapter

Published 2024 by Next Chapter

Cover art by Jaylord Bonnit

This book is a work of fiction. Apart from known historical figures, names, characters, places, and incidents are the product of the author's imagination. Other than actual events, locales, or persons, again the events are fictitious.

All rights reserved. No part of this book may be reproduced or transmitted in any form or by any means, electronic or mechanical, including photocopying, recording, or by any information storage and retrieval system, without the author's permission.

# 1

## 2010

"Cody, can you hear me, come in," Heath tried to regain contact with the commander of the Squad through the radio, but all that came through was static. Blackfire Island waited for any signs of life. several minutes felt like hours in the command center.

The eyes of the lower floors were glued to their various screens, sticking to their posts and doing their jobs, trying to find ways to reestablish communication with the team.

A voice cut through the endless static. "Alive," The signal was weak. "Someone clear that mess up," Heath ordered once it was reestablished. "Rizan is dead. The team is alive, no survivors. No one made it," Cody's voice came through the static in broken pieces. Heath narrowed his eyes. He didn't believe that. After all, they lived through it.

With no eyes on the situation, there was no choice but to trust them. He hated that. "Stand by, hold your position for pickup," Heath replied. He sat down and let out a sigh of relief as he picked up the phone beside him.

"Erin. Mission accomplished. Send the Aurora and get them home," Heath ordered and hung up. Of course, experience told him it was never over. He placed his hand back on the black phone again in anticipation of what came next.

Seconds later, the phone rang again, and he picked it up, rolling his eyes a few seconds later. "What do you mean did we get it? We are sending the chopper now. Your precious rock is MIA for now, and hopefully, it stays that way. No good can come of that thing," Heath said, trying to keep his temper.

"Zeron forces lost what was there. All your people would have died too if they went. I don't know how the Squad made it out alive or even what happened. I'm sure we'll get eyes on the situation soon. I'll send you the report when I get it. Tell your people to calm down. The crisis is over," Heath said and couldn't help but smile.

"Oh, you sent a file over. I'll look at it and talk to you later," Heath said, hung up the phone turned to a computer monitor to access his account. There was a file waiting for him as the Professor had said. It was marked "Cyranthis Stone Information." Not thinking twice, he opened it.

Twenty seconds later, every computer screen in the command center went black with a message in red: "This is what you get when you send the Syndicate lap dogs to a job meant for the Guardians. Call us next time."

"That bastard," Heath said. "I'm going to kill them all someday," he finished as his phone rang.

"Yes, I am aware that every system is down, Nick. Fix it. It's their idea of a prank. We need an upgrade anyway. A few more terabytes never killed anyone," Heath replied and stared at the black screen as he hung up the phone.

# 2

The chopper moved over the jungle. Smoke rose from a clearing below. Some of the primitive-looking buildings were on fire, but others were sinking into the ground, almost melding with the ground itself. The clearing was pitch black the earth had been burned by something strong enough to kill everything it touched.

"Our instruments are going insane. Do you see anyone down there?" one pilot said to the other.

"I don't see anything, but God, what happened down—wait. I see movement, five of them down there," the other man pointed towards the ground in their direction. On the ground, five men covered in blood and the black ash that covered the ground limped away from a building that burned with bright green fire.

The chopper landed. The side door slid open, and the five men wasted no time in climbing in. "Get us out of here," Cody said as he pressed the communication button on the side of the chamber. Dustin looked out over the hellish scene of twisted, burning buildings and closed the door as the chopper began to rise.

"What the hell was that back there?" Josh asked, his bleeding left hand covering a blackened piece of flesh on his right arm.

"I don't know. It's dead, it's all dead, and if we are lucky, we'll never have to go back," Wyatt replied. Blake stared at the floor. All he could think about was what he saw and was trying his best to forget all of it.

"If we're lucky, this was our one service. That's the deal, right? One big mission then retirement?" Blake asked, eyes not wavering.

"That's the plan," Josh replied, leaning back, grunting as his charred skin cracked while he moved.

"No more talking," Wyatt replied. It hurt to talk. It even hurt to listen right now.

The rest of the trip was made in silence. In a few hours—how many wasn't known to them as time was lost to their own personal thoughts—by the time they landed on Blackfire Island, they had recovered. The green light came on, and Cody opened the door and got out only to face their General standing there with arms crossed.

"Did you recover the stone?" he asked them as they got out.

"No, and it's better we didn't. That thing, whatever it was, isn't worth having," Cody replied as they started to walk to the door.

"What happened out there?" Heath asked as they walked around him. He turned around.

"Hell happened out there. I don't know, but it's over. You'd be better off not knowing. The stone, the Cyranthis cult, and everyone who was sent to that place is dead. I couldn't tell you why they died or how. All I can tell you is that everything burned when the golden light touched it. It will be in my report. I'll be sure not to leave anything out," Cody said and followed the others inside.

"I can't wait to read that. Hope it's longer than a page," Heath said and followed them inside.

"Maybe two pages," Cody replied as they walked through the door.

Wyatt got into his quarters and put his mud-covered sword across his lap as he sat on his bed. "Aren't you lucky? The others have to put their weapons in holding, but I get to take you with. Yeah, you're special or something," he said to his blade. "Let's get you cleaned up. Jungle mud and blood aren't a good look for you," he said, not wanting to get too comfortable. He got up and started the process to clean the blood off before he would take care of himself.

Dustin walked into his room and sat down on the bed. "Why?" he asked himself as the reality of what they did set in. Even here in the quiet, he could still hear all the screaming. "Just shut up," he said, reached over to the table beside his bed, opened a sliding door, and pulled out a bottle of deep red liquor. He twisted the cap off and swallowed a bunch of it.

"Just shut up," he said again, closing his eyes.

Josh moved into his room and punched the wall as soon as the door shut behind him. "They got off easy," he said, pulling his throbbing hand out of the dented metal wall. He could feel his broken knuckles pop back into place as he stretched his hand out. Josh wanted to make them suffer. It wasn't right that they all torched by some weird lightshow. As much as he wanted to go back and do it over, there was nothing to do now but clean up and do his best to move on.

Blake opened his door and looked down. There on the ground was the dime he left at the top of his door. "Someone was in my room," he said while picking it up. He scanned the room and saw that everything else was how he left it. Everything but a long black hair laying on the floor, he almost missed in the fluorescent light.

"Emily, what were you doing in my room?" he asked no one. He dropped the hair in the trash. It was a mystery for another day. Right now, he wanted to get cleaned up.

Cody walked inside his room and tore his already ripped-up

shirt off. It was so caked with blood that the thing broke as if it were frozen instead. He did his best not to think about it.

"Everyone's alive, mission success, man I'm good," he said. With a smile, he climbed into the shower. Before meeting back up with the others, he figured he'd call home to see how they were doing. It was always nice to connect with Mom and Dad.

It was a half hour later that the five of them met up in the briefing room at about the same time.

"So, who else never wants to do a Syndicate mission again?" Dustin asked.

"Yeah, it sucks, but it was our suck at least. Who's up for going home?" Cody asked.

"Hell yes," Wyatt said, sitting in a chair and leaning back, stretching with a big yawn.

"Yep, I'd say it's time to go home. Rule of one, we all made it and are home free, heroes forever," Josh said with sarcasm, but the word "heroes" didn't make any of them feel that great. They wouldn't call what they did heroic, only necessary.

Emily walked into the room and got all their attention at once. She held a silver case at her side. "Guys, you did well out there. Once I get your reports, we can send you all home. Of course, you all know the rules, and the Syndicate will take care of its own," she said as she sat down, took a strange-looking recording device out, set it on the table, and turned it on.

"Emily, what were you doing in my room?" Blake asked. Emily's eyes got wide for a second.

"It was a thirty-six-hour shift. I was walking down the hall and figured you wouldn't mind," she replied.

"Hey, what's wrong with my bed? You can sleep in my room anytime you want," Wyatt said with a slight chuckle. Emily rolled her eyes at the comment.

"I'll remember that for next time. Now, if we're done, we can get started," she replied. The five of them sat at the table. Their silence told her all she needed to know.

"And here we go," Emily said.

# 3

The unorthodox debrief lasted for four hours as each member told their version of the events. The last one to tell his story was the commander. After the last sentence was said, she shut off the device. After all the conversation, the silence felt weird. Emily took the initiative to break it.

"You all seem alright to me, considering what you went through. As always, this will go into the archives, classified of course. You men are free to go wherever you like. We will be in contact if we need you. Keep your phones," she said and placed the case on the table, opened it, and spun it around to reveal five black, average-looking smartphones.

"Each of you gets one. If it rings, pick it up. No one else will have this number but us. Go out and enjoy the world you just helped save. You earned it," she said and leaned back in her chair as each one took a phone, one by one, and looked at it for a second. "Those won't come out for a couple of years, so be sure to keep them out of sight. The tech boys tell me they'll be the next big thing," Emily said, and Wyatt tapped on the black screen.

"I can't see people being interested in anything this small," he replied. Then he slid it into his side pocket, and the others did too.

"So, that's it? We can go just like that?" Josh asked her because he figured there was more to it.

"Yep, that's all there is to it. I assumed you needed some alone time, so I arranged transport to take you back to the mainland. Five boats are waiting for you in the harbor. Get out of here before we change our minds," Emily said. It was hard to tell if she was serious or not as her eyes intensified their glare and her smile disappeared.

"Right, thank you. I think we'll be leaving," Cody said with a weak smile. He and the others got up and left the room. "So, that's what it feels like to do that," she said to herself. Emily smiled a little as she remembered when it was done to her and the rest of their team.

The five of them wanted to leave Blackfire Island for many reasons but mainly because the place itself was dangerous in a way unlike any other place on earth. They moved down the well-lit halls in silence, knowing the way toward the entrance to the harbor. Walking outside, the sudden change from the dull interior light to bright natural light made them flinch, but it didn't last long. The sun was lighting up the harbor and the black shoreline, making the ocean water sparkle. It looked like a painting.

In a few minutes, the light would fade as the 'mountain' of Blackfire Island blocked it, casting a grim shadow over everything, returning to its natural state. "Come on, let's go," Wyatt said as he walked toward five gray transport boats waiting for them.

The dock was old and appeared to be falling apart in places. If anyone knew anything about this place, it was a miracle they were able to get anything built here at all. The dark water was still, despite the gentle breeze.

"Yeah, let's get out of here. This place creeps me out," Dustin said, and the others couldn't help but agree with him. "See you guys later. Have fun, whatever it is you decide to do," Blake said and was the first to walk towards his boat. Despite the ancient appearance of the wooden structure, he didn't hesitate to cross it.

"Fun, right. I'll remember to do that. I hope I can still remember how to drive one of these things," Josh said and followed Blake. The last three didn't have anything to say, and they walked to their transports.

The boats sped together, side by side, for a few minutes after reaching the open sea. Cody looked to his right and left and nodded. The others returned the gesture. One by one, they pulled away from the group, fading into the distance, destination unknown.

# 4

## TWO YEARS LATER.

Nothing ever changed for the better. War still infested the world, and suffering only increased. Wyatt supposed the worst part of all was that the Cyranthis religion didn't wither and die like it was supposed to after its leader and his compound were wiped out. Still, the terrible feeling in his stomach that they missed something wasn't going to let him rest easy.

There was nothing he could do but sit here on the top of a skyscraper in Los Angeles, ignore the breeze through his thin black street clothes, and think about it. Lately, he had found himself becoming isolated from society. At the same time, he dreaded the idea of being alone in this twisted world. Now the high places of the world were the only retreat he had left that made him feel halfway normal.

His legs dangled over the edge, and his hands rested on the railing to keep people from falling off to their deaths as he mindlessly gazed into the endless sea of lights below him, a sea of orange starlight from the ground. His thoughts about failure, death, and leaving a job unfinished were shattered when someone else started to talk.

"Hey, you can't be up here," a deep voice said from behind

him, and Wyatt turned slightly to look at who it was. "Oh, look, it's security guard B," he said as he stood up.

"Fine, I'll leave," he replied as he looked over all the lights below. "Come with me, and we'll talk about this," the guard said as he realized then what was about to happen, and his deep voice lightened. Wyatt laughed at him and shook his head.

"If you even knew half the truth, it might be enough to drive you insane," Wyatt said, then without any warning, he jumped off the side of the building, much to the horror of the guard as he rushed to the edge and looked down to see the falling person, but he saw no one. "Damn it, what a waste," the security guard said and reached for his radio to report what had happened, but Wyatt's hand stopped him from behind.

"How did you? I saw you," was all he could get out before the guard passed out from shock where he stood. "Yeah, I get that a lot," Wyatt said as he caught the guy and dragged him back from the edge. He was about to leave when one of the brighter lights in the distance exploded. Even from here, Wyatt could see the dim flicker of the flames.

"What the hell is that?" he asked himself and took his phone out, the same one he'd gotten some time ago, and waited for it to ring. He looked from the phone to the distant flames and when it didn't ring, he figured that this had nothing to do with anything. "Oh well," Wyatt said with a shrug, then made his way back to the exit.

# 5

Dustin was in some nameless bar, trying to get wasted, but having a healing factor made it difficult. He was keeping to himself. The place was noisy enough, and it was what he was looking for.

The noise helped drown out the memories of battle. Too many nights he had nightmares of an ever-expanding golden light with faces of the dead within it. He was waking up in the night covered in sweat, and sometimes blood. He was never quite sure where the blood came from.

Sometimes he glanced up to see people walking by, enjoying themselves, and he hated it. He'd long since forgotten what it felt like to be happy, but he could pretend if he had to. The music was a strange electronic buzz that he didn't like, but it did the job well enough to keep the horror in his mind at bay.

The noise started to die out, and it was enough to make him more aware of his surroundings. He had no idea what time it was, but it wouldn't be the first time he lost time in a place like this.

At first, he felt as if the people were getting close to him for no reason, but then it was apparent that something was happening because it was the big screen TV they were all watching now. Something had happened, and he didn't want to know what it was.

The tender behind the bar turned up the volume and killed the music at the same time. Dustin couldn't help but pay attention to the news guy. Something told him he didn't want to see whatever it was on the screen, so he closed his eyes and listened. His grip got tighter on his bottle as the words from the television began.

"This is John Michaels reporting for KRGR news channel six out of Los Angeles. A bomb has gone off here at the Cyranthis Temple. The building was filled as they were getting ready to perform their midnight mass for their 'Festival of the Trucido' celebration. The building holds six hundred. As you can see behind me, firefighters are desperately trying to put out the flames but so far aren't having much luck in their efforts to contain this inferno," the man kept talking.

Dustin stopped paying attention, but he couldn't help but smile a little. The madness had caught on somehow, much like any other cult might, he supposed. He couldn't help but not feel sorry for the dead, but he wondered who else would know the truth well enough to know it was pure evil, or perhaps this was someone's way of getting attention.

Religion was a violent sport after all, and since Cyranthis began to rise, it also gave rise to the strange alliance of Christian and Muslim terrorists having a common enemy. The popular kids didn't like the new kid on the block taking all their attention.

Dustin found the whole thing amusing because he knew it would never end until people gave up killing for their ideas. Still, he had to admit to himself, six hundred dead Cyranthis worshippers was funny. He was careful because people were breaking down around him. Obviously, there had been some devoted people in the group.

"Oh, something is happening behind me," Michaels said in a surprised voice, and Dustin wondered what it could be now. He looked at the television along with the others at these words, and the camera focused in on the wreckage. Something was coming out of the fire. It looked like a man covered in metal. Dustin thought it was an illusion at first, too much to drink maybe. He rubbed his eyes and looked again but the vision remained the same.

The iron thing stepped toward the reporter. The heavy footsteps were loud, as the firemen looked on, unsure of what to do or what it was. Dustin couldn't take his eyes off the screen, but he knew this, whatever it was, wasn't going to play fair.

The thing towered over the newscaster as it looked. Its body was covered in metal, like its skin had turned into steel. Its eyes were bright blue as it looked into the camera. It must have been seven feet tall, at least. Dustin wasn't sure why, but it appeared that the metal was growing through the flesh. The waist down was pure steel, and the upper body was only halfway completed on the left side.

"We are here to eradicate this scourge from the earth. Cyran- this is a false god. Anyone who believes in its teachings or follows this abomination will be destroyed. This is a declaration of war," the iron man said to the newscaster. Then it put his left hand through the man's chest with ease. The blood spilled for everyone to see. Dustin didn't flinch while the rest of the crowd recoiled in audible horror.

The thing turned to look at the nameless cameraman who was still filming, too scared to run, or too stupid. A dark hand came over the screen as it reached forward, and the TV went to a generic 'please stand by' screen, black with big white letters, and the droning monotone sound came from the speakers.

All at once, the crowd began to panic. Someone screamed out in the back, "The invasion is here." Invasion of what, Dustin wasn't sure. He hoped it wasn't aliens.

When whoever screamed that the invasion had started, the former crowd of partygoers went over the edge into a relentless rush for the exit of the place. Everyone had a plan for when the world ended, and now was their chance to do whatever they believed would work for the best.

Dustin didn't panic at the news that the world might be coming to an end as he finished his bottle under the notice of the crowd rushing to get out around him. He looked at his phone, pulled it from his pocket as he expected it to ring, but it didn't. Dustin thought to himself, then decided to make a call of his own. He dialed a number and waited for him to pick up the phone.

Blake picked up the other end.

"Hey, did you see the news?" Dustin asked him, then shook his head. "Yes, I know the news is all bad, but stop watching all those stupid car shows and turn it to the news. Literally any other, real, station," Dustin said. "How did I get this number? I messed with the phone, didn't you?" Dustin asked, already annoyed.

"No, I didn't get a phone call. I expected one, and why do you watch all those stupid car shows anyway? You could have any of them, it seems stupid if you ask me," Dustin asked, and Blake hung up. "Good talking to you too, Blake," Dustin said and stood up, the place was empty now. It didn't take long to clear out. He took one last look at that television screen, still on the standby screen.

"Looks like I am going to Los Angeles. I hate Los Angeles," Dustin said while he put his coat on.

He walked behind the bar, ignoring the bartender, and grabbed the biggest bottle of whiskey he could see. "You can't take that," the woman said. "The world's ending, didn't you see the TV? Take a couple for yourself, lock up, and go home before the looters raid the place," Dustin replied as he walked out into the cold air, cracking the bottle open at the same time.

## 6

Blake hung up the phone without answering Dustin, changed it to the local news channel, and saw what Dustin was talking about. "Coming to you as soon as we can bring you more information, all we know is that a mysterious terrorist group has declared war against the Cyranthis religion. For those of you just joining us, we will replay the declaration of war as it was displayed. A warning, the footage is extremely graphic and is not suitable for children," the newswoman said. Then they cut to the footage of the newscaster being killed by the metal thing.

"What's the big deal, Dustin? They just want Cyranthis worshippers, good for them, who cares?" Blake said and was about to change the channel back to his favorite car show, *Gearhead*. Blake hated this religion and thought that eradicating it would be a good deal for everyone. On the other hand, something about the metal person didn't sit well with him.

"War? You picked the wrong country to do that in, metal guy," he said and figured if this problem were serious enough the Syndicate would give him a call. He turned it back to his show and waited for the call to come in. He didn't feel compelled to do anything he didn't have to. Even with his show on, he knew the others were going to feel like doing something about this mess and he would be dragged into it, too.

So much for the Rule of One, but who knows, maybe they already had a replacement team and forgot to say anything. Blake supposed he would find out.

# 7

Ever since returning from the mission, Josh watched the spread of this religion as if it were a virus. He was determined to bring it down, expose it for the evil it was. Tonight was the beginning of their Trucido Festival week. The first midnight mass was for members only. Cyranthism was strange and new to the world. This Festival had been advertised for months in the religion, but it was still a mystery to most of the world at large. There were many theories on the internet.

Tonight, he was going to break in after the thing was to start to find out more. He had begun to make his approach toward the building when something came out of the sky and smashed into the building.

The whole thing exploded with enough force to kill everyone inside. Josh was sent flying back into someone's car, shattering the glass on impact and caving the side in. Josh waited a few seconds before trying to move. It was too painful to try now. This would have killed anyone else. "Guess I got lucky, but what the hell?" he said. For a time, all he did was watch the flames and listen to the screaming of those unlucky enough not to have been killed by the initial blast.

It wasn't long before a new sound was coming his way—

sirens of all kinds, and that was his signal to get clear of the scene. He pulled himself out of the wreckage and stood up, brushing all the glass from his clothes. "I liked these clothes, too. Thanks, random missile attack," he said.

He was bleeding from somewhere, but that wouldn't last long. He started to limp away from the scene to find a quiet place to recover while still being able to see everything. He searched for unlocked cars to break into so he could find a place to sit down and heal. He was quite sure no one in the parking lot was going to need any of their cars anytime soon. He found one that was big enough for him and had a great view of everything that was happening.

The cops and firefighters arrived first, then the news people showed up, at least one of them did a few minutes later. "Wow, they sure are fast, they should be delivering pizzas. Thinking about it, I sure could use a pizza," Josh said as he pulled out a shard of glass from his arm and tossed it away.

All he could do was watch. He saw the newscaster there, saying something into the camera, but what caught his attention was the thing coming from the flames. "What?" he asked as he got out of the car to get a better look and could see the flames reflecting off the metal body from here. It was disturbing.

He watched as the thing dispatched the news guy for no reason. This made him angry enough to want to do something. The Syndicate code said he didn't exist. "Screw the code," he said and began to run back to the scene.

"Sir, what in the hell is that thing?" Officer Watts said to his partner as they noticed the reporter get slaughtered. "I don't know, but I'm not going to tell it to freeze first," his partner said, and the two of them drew their weapons and began to fire at it after it crushed the cameraman with his own camera.

The rest of the cops didn't need to ask what was going on as they saw the two dead people at the feet of this metal monster and started to shoot. All the bullets did was attract the thing's attention. "Do you think this is a good idea? I mean, it doesn't seem to be falling and—" Watts was cut off by the superior officer.

"It's just some kind of body armor. Aim for the joints and the head, we'll take it down, you'll see," he replied. The seven police officers kept firing, and the thing marched in their direction, not bothered by the bullets. "This is a bad idea, maybe we should have tried talking to it before we shot at it and—" Watts was cut off again. "Talking is always a bad idea, son, it didn't do that reporter any good, it won't do us any good either. Retreat, call for backup," the superior officer ordered as he stopped shooting and broke rank.

Watts looked at the machine in time to see its eyes turn from blue to red and fire two thin red beams in their direction. The beams struck one of their squad cars and it exploded, the body of the car flying into the air and landing on top of another car, crushing it.

This made Josh stop in his tracks. There was no way he wanted to test his healing factor against a direct hit from whatever that was. He needed to make a better plan than the one he had now.

Josh ran to the firemen who were unaware of what was going on due to their own situation. He ran to a man who looked in charge. "Hey, you, you've got to listen to me," Josh said, taking the uniformed man with the white helmet by the shoulders and spinning him around without thinking about it. Others rushed in and grabbed Josh and pulled him back with difficulty.

"Listen to you, calm down before you get yourself hurt. Were you in the blast? Who are you?" the chief asked, and Josh was quick to respond. "Look over there, there is something bad coming this way and we have to stop it," Josh said as he pulled himself free from the two holding him back. The chief looked and his eyes got wide then as he saw the squad cars on fire and something inhuman approaching.

"You've got to soak that thing with all the pressure you can get on it," Josh said. The chief didn't respond, not knowing what to make of what was coming towards them. "Damn it man, listen to me right now. Get your hoses on this thing and get the rest of your people out of here. I'll help. Can you do this?" Josh asked again then and turned to look at the closing-in metal thing behind him.

"Yes, I can do this. Hose crew with me, everyone else evacuate the area," he ordered. The men looked at one another for a second before taking off in the other direction. Whatever this thing was, it was beyond their level to deal with. There was no reason to stick around. The chief pulled up his radio and began to issue orders. "You men on the hose, I need you to look over here. I need you to hose something down," he said in a hurry, and the four men on the hoses in the distance turned to look. Once they saw the metal thing moving in their direction, there didn't need to be any more orders.

They all changed direction, shutting off their water as they did in order not to spray one another. Josh pulled the fire chief out of the way while he was still trying to figure out what it was. It was so much closer now. "Let it have rip," someone yelled.

Josh watched as the fire hoses let their water go in four streams. Each one was a direct hit, but the metal infested man did not slow down. Josh was kind of impressed.

"Damn, I hoped that would work. Alright, Chief, you need to get your people out of here. As soon as I take this thing down, get the rest of them out of here too," Josh said and started to run at the new enemy before the chief could ask any questions.

Josh ran as fast as he could toward his enemy and didn't have time to think his plan through or wonder about some of the life choices he tended to make on the way there. He waited until the last possible second before he jumped over the impact zone, through the backsplash of the high-pressure water, and put his left forearm into the throat of the thing. The two locked eyes for a split second before Josh's added force tipped it off balance and the two of them fell through the air.

Josh made sure to be on top when it fell to the ground as the water drenched them both.

"Who are you?" the machine asked. "Insane apparently," Josh said and almost smiled before he was taken by the throat and thrown to the side with more force than he'd ever experienced in his life. He sailed through the air. He didn't know how far he traveled but came to a sudden stop as he crashed into something metal. It caved in and brought him to a stop.

Josh saw that the firefighters and cops had gotten away. It was all he was trying to do. Everything went black. The last thing he heard was his phone starting to ring before he gave in to the creeping unconsciousness.

# 8

Cody cancelled the phone call. No answer made him worry that Josh was already in the middle of things because that would be the only reason he wouldn't answer. That idiot brother of his was always getting into trouble. He walked out of his house and sat on the porch to try and forget the chaos that was going on tonight.

He didn't need to know what was going on past what the television was reporting. The Syndicate would let them know if they were needed or not. It was the way the Squad had always been, and he was sure that it wasn't about to change anytime soon.

The natural sounds of the countryside at night didn't distract him from his thoughts. He couldn't help but wonder who was behind all of this. A machine person wasn't familiar to him beyond stories and movies that involved confusing time travel elements. There weren't any enemies left that he knew about, and they took care of all the major threats. This had to be somebody new, which was the only explanation.

Cody could almost admire the mind who came up with the idea of going to war with the Cyranthis people. To him, they were all crazy and dangerous, but when he watched that reporter get killed on television, he wondered if there wasn't more to the attack.

There was no point in wondering. He knew there was always more to it, or maybe the reporter was a member of the new cult. It was impossible to know anything. Cody was willing to go check this situation out, but the code was official. If you weren't called by the Syndicate, you weren't supposed to do anything, and so far, his phone remained silent.

He thought about trying to call his team, but he wasn't in any hurry to do that yet.

Looking up at the stars and listening to the wind through the trees was much better. He would wait for his phone to ring. Until then, it was quiet. Just the way he liked it.

# 9

Heath was in his office, reviewing some files for other projects when Erin rushed in. "Sir, you need to see this," she said. Heath didn't like her worried tone. He got up and walked the short distance into the command center where the news was already on the main screen and a map of Los Angeles showed other disturbances taking place in real time in the form of red dots in various places.

"What do we know?" Heath asked then and tried to take it all in.

"Not much, but it looks metal, machine we think. It demolished the Cyranthis temple and everyone inside," Erin replied.

"Are the Guardians responsible?" Heath asked.

"No. They contacted us seeing if this was us," she replied. Heath kept his cool.

"Tell them it's not us, at least I hope it's not us," he said as the phone on his belt rang. He picked it up, knowing who it was already.

"What do you mean, you want them? The armor, sir I don't think—" Heath was cut off.

He paused for a minute. "It's still experimental, the armor won't be ready for years at least, no one has used it for anything," Heath said. On the other end of the phone, somebody started to scream various threats Erin could hear despite being some distance away trying to monitor the situation.

"Yes sir. They'll be activated," Heath said and sighed as he hung up the phone and looked at Erin. "Go get Emily, get the armors ready for teleportation. War has come to America, and we were caught sleeping on the job."

Erin was about ready to argue against teleporting, but the glare from Heath made her think twice about it. He wasn't in a good mood, and there was no reason to make it any worse. She left the command center.

She ran down the halls of the complex to Emily's quarters. Erin stopped at the metal door and tried to open it, but something was wrong with the keypad. It wasn't responding to the code.

Erin became frustrated and slammed her fist against the door. "Wake up, we are under attack, and we have work to do." She hoped it was getting through the metal.

"If I have to cut this door down, you'll be sorry. I'll have you on diagnostic duty for a month!" she screamed at the door, and that did the trick. The door slid open. Emily was standing there, sleep in her eyes and hair a mess.

"What is it? Who's attacking what?" she asked, still trying to wake up.

"I don't know. Machine people, at best guess. Heath wants the armors prepped and ready to go—" Emily shook her head then and stopped her.

"You built the stupid things. You do it. I'm going back to bed," she said and started to turn around.

"I meant prepped for teleportation," Erin said, and it was enough to stop Emily in her tracks.

"What in the hell is going on out there? You get those armors ready, and I'll—I'll figure something out. I'll need five minutes," Emily said and slid the door shut.

"Five minutes, nothing ever takes five minutes, but alright," Erin said to no one and rushed towards the armor room.

"Does anyone ask if I am done testing this? No, of course not. Get the armor ready, they said. I don't even know if it works right." She was complaining, but no one expected killer robots. She supposed it was why they called it a surprise attack.

The doors opened with a hiss. It didn't attract the attention of anyone who was working in the room at the time, various people in green lab coats running tests on different projects.

"Alright, everyone listen up. The powers that be require our assistance. I want these armors ready to go within the hour. Prep them and make no mistakes because mistakes cost lives," Erin said. At once, the various workers stopped what they were doing and got to work.

Erin couldn't help but wonder what the future held as they got the armors ready. They were a big maybe. For all the things that could go right, a million more could fail. She did her best not to think about it.

She hoped that this day would never come. Would there ever be a weapon created by people that would never have to be used in combat? She doubted it. Now it was time to do what she was supposed to do. No time to waste because disaster was on the move, and it waited for no one.

# 10

Cody was under the stars on his porch as the cold December wind blew across it. His phone rang, he took a breath, then he picked it up. "Well, hello General." Cody gazed off into the vast nothing as he spoke. "Yes, I know what is going on. I do have television. What is the situation?" Three simple words made him feel uncomfortable. "What do you mean you don't know? You had one job," Cody said, frustrated now, and stood up.

"Yeah, I can be there, but it will take an hour, maybe more, depending on traffic." Cody winced after that. "General, I get you're scared, but shut up. You're being pathetic. Don't worry, I won't tell anyone," Cody said and hung up the phone before the General could reply.

Cody looked back at his house. It was a small blue house in the middle of nowhere. There was nothing in it he couldn't go without or miss. So, he turned around and walked towards his truck without bothering to lock the door, not caring if someone broke into it or not. He started his green truck and drove away towards whatever fate was waiting for him.

Wyatt was in the elevator, listening to some generic elevator music to some vague and familiar song he couldn't quite name.

That strange explosion he saw was bugging him. He wondered what was going on. It was about then his phone rang, and he picked it up.

"Hello." It was a formality. He knew who it was. "I saw the explosion. I needed some alone time. I didn't know what it was, but you say it was the Cyranthis Temple. Why should I care about a bunch of dead crazy people?" Wyatt was annoyed once the news was delivered but listened anyway. "A machine did it? Well, that sounds interesting. Maybe we can help him take down this stupid religion, and then after we're finished, we can go after the rest of them. The world would be better off." Wyatt's day was turning bad. He was annoyed with all things that involved religion.

"I know the place. I can be there, but do we have a plan here, or are we going to meet up and share old war stories?" Wyatt said and waited. "A surprise? Fine, I'll be there. I like surprises." Wyatt said and hung up the phone, put it away. "But I hate reunions." He looked up at the speaker, still trying to figure out what that song was.

Dustin was on the street walking away from the bar at night. There were usually few people out, but now the news of the invasion on the news had chaos beginning to appear. People were out in the streets, loading up their cars in places while other places, normally busy, felt quiet. Dustin didn't care about any of this and picked up his phone as it rang.

"Well, hello General. Did you see the evil machine thing on television? Because I did. It looked like it was something that escaped from Fort DIAB from the stories I've heard," Dustin said as he kept walking down the street. "I can get there. I'll need a car," he said as he stopped walking and looked around.

"Yeah, I already called Blake, but he didn't seem interested in talking to me. You should call him. You work on this, and I'll find some wheels. I assume the others are going to be there too?" Dustin asked and didn't smile when he got his answer. "Alright, I will be there as soon as I can," he said, hung up, and spotted a rather nervous-looking man running back and forth from a building, packing things into his car as fast as he could.

"You'll do," Dustin said and walked up behind this panicked man as he was packing things in the back of his station wagon. Dustin took a big swig of his bottle. "Hey buddy, that wagon got a full tank?" he asked, pretending to do his best drunk impression he could. The man turned around and saw the bottle. "Get out of here, I have a gun," he said. Dustin could see the panic in his eyes. The ring on the finger, he had to protect someone inside the house.

"Oh, a gun. That sucks for me," Dustin replied, taking another big drink, wincing and staggering to the right a little, but still moving forward at an uneven pace.

"You're drunk, not stupid. Get off my lawn," Dustin didn't see any guns. "You're right," Dustin replied, and everything about him changed. He rushed forward, grabbed the man by the shirt collar, and in the same motion, spun around and put the man's head into the hood of the wagon. The man was knocked out cold.

"Sorry, but I need this more than you do," Dustin said as he laid him on the ground.

Dustin then proceeded to remove all the guy's stuff. It took a few seconds to do, and he laid it next to his victim. Dustin shut the back hatch, walked to the driver's side, and was happy to see the keys were already in the ignition.

He got into the car, put the bottle in the passenger seat. Checked the back seat to make sure there weren't any kids. Once he saw it was clear, he started it and drove down the street.

"I can't show up in this thing. I'll never hear the end of it," Dustin said as he drove down the road, not worried about the cops. He was sure they were about to have bigger problems.

Blake's show was finishing, and as he was reaching for the remote to change it to his second favorite show, 'Unicorn Hunter X,' his phone rang again. "Twice in one night, really?" Blake asked and picked it up, expecting Dustin.

"I said—" And he was cut off. "Los Angeles? Even under the best conditions I couldn't get there until midnight," he said, still holding the remote in his other hand. "Two hours at the most. Are the others going to be there?" he asked, setting the remote down on the table beside him. "Great. Any word on what the plan is, or is it all going to be a surprise?" Blake asked and shut the television off.

"A surprise? I hate surprises, but just because I like you, I'll show up." Then he hung up, didn't care if it was orders or not, he liked to pretend that he had some say in the matter.

He stood up and had two things to do before he left. First, he needed to get dressed because shorts and a t-shirt weren't going to cut it. It was a quick two minutes for him to throw on some jeans, and he decided to keep the same black shirt on. The second thing he had to decide was what car he wanted to drive. Heath sounded worried. Blake could tell when someone was trying to keep their cool under pressure. It was no time to take it slow.

Blake had always liked to live life in the fast lane, and that addiction only got worse since he'd made it into the Delta Squad. He walked out to his garage and turned on the light. He had three cars to pick from, all of them he'd kill to protect from anyone. He needed speed, and after five seconds of consideration, he chose the silver Viper SRT. Working for the Syndicate had its perks.

He opened the garage door as he got in his chosen car. In the back of his mind, he knew that wherever he was going, it might mean never coming back here again.

He looked to the left and the right of him, admired his small but elite collection, and pulled out of the garage. He was long gone before the garage door was even closed. Blake knew that he had a long way to go and not a lot of time to get there.

## 11

Wyatt was the first to arrive. The meeting spot was a parking lot. In the distance was some stadium. It was blue and surrounded by white, Greek-inspired pillars. Wyatt looked at it for some time. He didn't know who might have played there and didn't care. The sounds of sirens filled the night air in all directions, and since the Syndicate made this their meeting place, he was sure whatever passed as security around here would have been taken care of.

He had no idea when the others were going to show up, but he knew it wouldn't be a long wait. Wyatt didn't know what to expect. There was a display in the distance. All Wyatt could read on it were two things:

What day it was and the time. December 19th, 2012. Midnight. He looked away towards the entrance and saw a pair of headlights coming in his direction. A brown station wagon was moving in his direction, and it only took a minute to clear the distance. Wyatt walked in the same direction.

"Dustin, is that you?" Wyatt asked and laughed as he did. Dustin opened the door. "Listen, I won't tell anyone you showed up in that, but for the story to stick, you should park over there or something, right?"

"Right, I suppose I should," Dustin replied, got back in and drove off. Wyatt noticed another pair of headlights pulling into the lot seconds later, a green truck. Wyatt watched as, even though the entire place was empty, the truck still parked perfectly between the lines. "Wouldn't want to break the rules or anything," Wyatt said, rolling his eyes.

Cody got out of the truck and closed the door. He was careful not to slam the door. "Dustin showed up too, but for some reason, he's parking way down there," Wyatt said and shrugged. "That kid just isn't right. I don't think I'll ever figure him out," Cody said and shook his head. "I tried calling Josh, but he didn't pick up. He's either dead or waist deep in someone else's blood. Either way, I am sure it's something I'll be blamed for." Cody said, and Wyatt laughed at him because he knew it was true.

Dustin was already halfway back and noticed that Cody was here and was happy to see him but wasn't sure why, so he waved. "You're right, Dustin isn't normal," Wyatt said as he shook his head while he waved.

The sound of an engine interrupted them, and without even looking, they knew only Blake, the one guy of the team who valued being invisible over anything, would show up in a car that would attract the most attention.

They turned as the silver Viper pulled up with no regard for parking spaces whatsoever. Blake shut his car off and got out. "So, think you could draw any more attention? Maybe if the car was on fire, more people would notice us?" Wyatt asked.

"Hey, don't judge me, man. There is a good chance I'll be killed doing whatever it is we are supposed to be doing. Why make the trip in some old pile like this?" he asked while motioning towards Cody's truck. "Gotta live a little, you know?" Blake said as he closed the door. Dustin walked up and glanced at the car. If he didn't say anything, maybe he wouldn't either. It was worth a shot.

"So, most of us are here. Any idea on what we do now, or did someone bring a picnic basket? Maybe this is a Syndicate prank or something," Wyatt said, already becoming restless at standing here.

"Calm down, knife boy, did you see that thing? I saw it. I think it's an alien, a robot alien," Dustin said to Wyatt. "Right," Wyatt replied.

"Yep, a robot thing declared war on a bad religion, so what? Doesn't this make things better?" Blake asked. "Yeah, that's what I'm saying. We should make some popcorn and let it do its thing, who cares?" Wyatt added. Dustin crossed his arms. He was going to say something, but Cody took over.

"No one has heard from Josh. Come on, someone please tell me you heard from him," Cody said, getting worried about his brother being missing in action. It was unlike him to be willing to miss a fight like this. Cody could tell by the look in their eyes they didn't know anything either.

Then their phones began to vibrate, and they all pulled them out. Their screens were lit up blue, and red words were on them.

'Locked on' it read, and the four of them looked around, unsure of what to say about it. No one had a chance to say anything when a bright blue light appeared behind them. They turned around to see something they had never seen before. Four capsules were on the pavement, each a different color. "Mega Man X?" Wyatt asked himself.

Then Cody's phone rang once and automatically turned on in speaker mode. "Hey, guys," Erin's voice came over the phone.

"With any luck, your packages have arrived. I will keep this short. The packages are the Vindicator class armor. First of their kind and might kill you once activated. We tested it a little but have no idea how any of this is going to work. Here is the rundown. Dustin, you get the orange one. I painted it myself. The Flame Genesis armor is exactly how it sounds. Heavy amounts of firepower and it can take a hit, feel free to experiment," she said and continued. Dustin looked at it. "Cool."

"Wyatt, you get the black one. The Hell Razor armor is the fastest, but try to stay out of too many fire fights. Don't worry, I put your sword with it," she said, and Wyatt had a sigh of relief. He missed his blade more than he thought he would.

"Blake, you get the white one. The Dead Eyes armor was made with stealth and targeting capabilities in mind. I saved the best for last. I think you'll like it if it doesn't kill you," she said. Blake shrugged it off. A little death didn't scare him.

"Cody, you get the blue one. A specially designed nanotech armor powered with plasma energy equipped with a one of a kind plasma cannon, use it wisely," Erin said. This rundown gave almost no information, and they all had questions.

"I have created a nanite ammo system, so for these armors, their ammo is unlimited, but a warning: If you overextend your power base, you will need to recharge. The armors draw ambient energy from nearly any energy source over time, so be aware of your surroundings always," she said, then continued.

"They don't fix themselves, so please don't break them if you can help it. Orders are simple: Find the machine and destroy it. I honestly don't know why you need these armors. It wasn't my choice," she said.

"This mission should take up to three hours to complete. Don't wear the armor longer than that if you can help it. We can't teleport it with you in it, so exit it when you're done, and we'll bring it back home. Physical contact activates the process, and as always, do your best to stay out of sight, stick to the rooftops. I have no idea how you're going to stay out of sight. Well, good luck," Erin finished, and the phone turned off.

"Where's Josh?" Cody asked, but it was too late. "Damn," he said and put his phone away.

## 12

"Armor suits? How are we supposed to work in these stupid things?" Blake asked, walking up to the white capsule that was taller than he was and reached out and touched it. At once, the metal oval shifted its pieces in seconds to reveal a white suit of armor that was open, but none of them could quite tell how to get into it. "They got the size wrong. This is way too big," Blake said, looking at the thing.

With no warning, Wyatt pushed Blake forward into the armor, and they all watched as it closed around him. The others took a step back to watch what was going to happen.

"Did you have to do that?" Cody asked Wyatt. "Yes," he replied, never taking his eyes off the armor.

Blake was concealed in darkness. Then there was a beep somewhere in the black, and things began to light up. A menu in red in front of him ran through a list too fast for him to read. Then the darkness gave way to what he saw before. He looked at his hands and saw they were bone white, but this armor had no weight to it. It was as if he was wearing nothing at all.

Blake looked up, and his armor scanned everything as he looked at it, telling him the distance between him and strategic vantage points. Blake turned around and faced the others. The armor scanned the three of them. Blake laughed when one by one their threat level came up in red: 'extremely high.'

"Guys, I don't know, but I don't feel any different at all. I mean, what I mean is you've got to try this," Blake said, and with a thought, a section on his back opened and he pulled out a sniper rifle, one of the most alien-looking ones he'd ever seen in his life. Blake wanted some practice and looked around. In the distance, he saw a brown station wagon and without thinking, took aim and fired.

The shot was surprisingly quiet, and the bullet sailed into the car but didn't make it to the other side.

He believed he heard Dustin say something that sounded like "Wait, don't shoot," but the car exploded into flames as he did.

"An exploding sniper bullet, how awesome is that?" Blake asked as he turned around to see Dustin's fist fill his vision and stop. He didn't feel a thing and was pushed back slightly. "Why in the hell did you shoot my car? I planned on returning it, you know?" Dustin yelled. It was easy to tell how angry he was as he gripped his right hand in pain from the impact.

"I was going to give it back," he said as he looked at the fire in the distance. Depressed, Blake decided to use that as target practice. Also, it wasn't subtle either. That explosion started a clock before people started to investigate, if anyone was looking at all.

"No more time to waste, let's suit up and take care of whatever this is so we can get back home," Cody said and knew it was time to get this show on the road. The three of them approached their capsules and within seconds repeated the same process.

"Not the typical uniform, too bulky if you ask me. How are we not supposed to be seen with these?" Wyatt asked as he tried to inspect himself. Wyatt's armor was smaller than the others. The armor was jet black with traces of gold in it, and Wyatt had no idea why. Despite being smaller than the others, he could tell it was made for speed. It looked fast in the inner holographic display. The only thing on this armor he knew well was the Hell Razor blade he had come to rely on.

It was in a sheath that was in the back of the armor, and he pulled it out. Despite the hand that held the blade being black and metal, he could somehow still feel it as if it were his own hand of flesh and bone. He waved it through the air twice, and it felt normal.

"I am not sure how they did this, but I am willing to give it a chance," Wyatt said as he looked around at the others, wondering what was going through their minds now.

Dustin looked at the flaming, but stolen, car in the distance and was not amused. Dustin turned and looked at the silver sports car and activated his weapon. From the top of his left arm, the barrel of a minigun emerged and began to spin.

"Hey, look. Target practice," Dustin said and fired his weapon and watched Blake's Viper get torn to expensive scrap metal in seconds.

"I like this gun," Dustin said as pieces of the Viper were still sliding across the lot. Blake was speechless as he watched Dustin turn one of his favorite cars into scrap metal. "You son of a bitch," Blake never finished as he leapt towards Dustin in a fit of rage.

The intentions were clear, but Dustin turned and put his right arm into Blake's stomach and sent him flying back. It was soon apparent who the stronger of the two was. Blake hit the ground and caused sparks to fly before he came to a stop. "You shot my car, so I shot yours," Dustin said as Blake got up.

"We are nowhere near even," Blake said and pointed his sniper rifle at him, but Dustin didn't budge. Cody stepped forward and put his left hand around the barrel of the gun and lowered it. "Knock it off, you two, we can settle this later. Right now, we have a job to do," Cody said, and Blake turned away, pulling his gun free. "Yeah, later sounds good to me," Blake said.

"Any idea on where to go first? We are kind of far away from anything," Wyatt said, changing the subject. "I know where to start. We need to go find that machine. What the hell do you mean, where do we go first? Use your head, man," Blake said and walked away. "I know you're upset, but you don't need to take it out on me," Wyatt replied and started walking with him, putting his sword away.

"Dustin, I hate to say this, but I think Blake is going to kill you. Watch your back out there," Cody said as he walked by. Knowing that if Blake wanted to take revenge on Dustin, there wouldn't be much he could do to stop him. "I'll be fine," Dustin replied and retracted his weapon, too.

## 13

Josh was woken up by the distant sound of a ringing phone. The thing he felt first was the pain. His right shoulder had a steel rod pushed all the way through it from behind. He opened his eyes and looked at it. All he could do was reach for the phone with his broken left hand. With a great amount of effort, he managed to answer it. He was healing but because it was taking so long to heal, he knew that he was damaged far more than he realized.

"Talk fast, this phone is heavier than it looks," Josh said as he struggled to hold it to his head.

"I'm stuck here. Impaled to a pile of metal and I am sure people will be showing up any minute. I don't know what you're talking about but don't send it here. Call back in a few minutes," Josh said and put the phone down as he dropped his arm and looked at the metal spike holding him where he was.

He reached over and took hold of the blood-covered spike and had no idea how deep into the wreck it went but had to take the chance.

He took a deep breath and pulled as hard as he could manage, and to his surprise, the spike slid through his flesh as he pulled out the spike with a great deal of pain and dropped it to the ground with a muffled clang.

Blood began to pour from the wound, and Josh put his hand over, putting pressure on it to stop the bleeding. He knew it would stop on its own, but it was a natural reaction. He wanted to lay here and rest for a few seconds, but the sirens were coming back in his direction, and he knew he needed to be anywhere else but here.

Josh sat up and took his hand off the wound, wiped his blood off on his jeans the best he could, grabbed his phone, and stood up. He didn't feel too much pain in his legs but was careful in case they were broken not to make it worse.

Josh rose from his bloody pit of broken steel and glass, looked around for a place to go. To his right, there was a parking ramp that looked to be perfect, and he started to walk in that direction as fast as his injured body would allow him to move, leaving a diminishing trail of blood as he walked.

His phone began to ring before he was halfway there. He answered it again.

"What armor are you talking about? I am heading towards a parking ramp. I'm not in the mood for climbing, so send it to the first level. I will be there soon enough," Josh said and peered into the dark interior of the ramp as a blue flash lit up the night for a second towards the back.

"I saw it. Heading there now," Josh said as he threw the phone to the side, annoyed with it already. Josh walked into the parking ramp, and there he saw a red and black capsule. Beside it was a plastic-wrapped package with a note on it.

Josh walked to the package, picked it up, and read the note. *You're going to need some new clothes. You're welcome.* Josh wasted no time in tearing off his blood-soaked clothes, opening the package, and finding the Syndicate had sent him a black outfit. He figured the Syndicate had some kind of obsession with the color black and wasn't quite sure why.

Not worried about it anymore, he walked to the capsule and

tried to figure it out. He walked around it and couldn't find an opening, and when he couldn't, he got frustrated, so he punched it. The second his fist made impact, the whole thing began to shift form into more of a humanoid shape right in front of him. Josh looked at it and wasn't quite sure what to do.

"Well, I guess they know what they are doing, so what the hell, give it a shot," he said and was unsure about this but decided to go for it anyway.

He took a deep breath and walked forward into the open armor, and as he did, the suit closed around him. For a few seconds, Josh was in complete darkness. He heard a small beep, and with that sound, his surroundings returned to him.

"Welcome to Vindicator class one armor. Code name Flesh Tearer. How may I help you today?" a computer voice asked him as he looked at his hands.

"Where is the rest of the squad?" he asked as he continued to test his range of movement. A map appeared on his visor with four dots indicating the others.

"They are two miles away from you and moving towards the primary target. You are closer, and it is recommended you wait for backup," it said in its monotone voice.

"Yeah, tell me about this armor, the quick version, and tell me where this enemy is. Give me a good route to avoid walking down a main street in front of everyone," he said and waited.

"Josh, you have the strongest armor of the five. Your weapons are dual miniguns, one on each wrist. You have a stealth mode for what it's worth. Just keeps you quiet. Your guns are powered by a nano regeneration system, you won't run out of bullets, but you run the risk of overheating the barrels. You have a zip line that makes getting to the rooftops easier, you'll need that. Is there anything else you'd like to know, or can we get to work now?" the computer asked him, and Josh looked around as the computer plotted out a path.

"Yeah, we have stuff to do. Tell the others I'm not dead, but if you can manage it, make it so they can see where I am if you could, thanks." Josh said and took his first step and was impressed. He could feel the hard ground under him as if he were wearing shoes. It was hard to tell he was wearing anything at all, and he realized he didn't know what he looked like. He walked back outside, looked up at the top level of the ramp.

"Going up," he said, raised his left arm, and fired his zip line towards the wall and watched as it connected. "Yeah, I don't trust this," Josh said as the black wire pulled him straight up. In three seconds, he was at the top of the ramp and pulled himself over the edge. Josh did his best to catch his breath. That was a rush and a little fun, too.

In the distance, there was a building that was on fire, and this was where the computer's path went. Also, to Josh, it appeared to be an impossible distance to cross.

"How am I supposed to make it that far without being seen?" Josh asked.

"Well, you start running, and then you jump off the edge. When I tell you, you fire the zip line where I am marking it. Follow the path, like this," the computer said and, to assist him, lit up a yellow path with a blue target on the burning building across from him. "Oh, so, kind of like Spider-Man," he said. The computer didn't seem to know or care about that.

Without thinking anymore about it, he took off running across the lot as fast as he could, and within seconds, he found himself moving faster than he'd ever moved before in his life.

He got to the edge and didn't time his jump well enough and smashed through the cement wall, but it didn't slow him down. Midway into the jump, he shot his line again and watched as the black cord hooked itself into the distant wall, pulling him towards it. He pulled himself up and stood on the burning building.

He looked towards the direction where his enemy was at, and the yellow path led him. "Having you around would have made life a lot easier in the other mission, you know?" he said to the computer, but it didn't respond. Josh wanted another crack at this strange enemy, so he took off running where the path was leading him.

So, he repeated the process again. Jumping between rooftops until the path came to an end after a few minutes. He was a bit sad it was over so fast. Jumping like that was the most fun he had in a while.

Josh looked down on the scene below and couldn't figure out what he was seeing at first. SWAT teams had a blockade around the machine, but it wasn't moving or saying anything. He thought it might have run out of power.

"Josh, I know you can see the situation. Don't do anything stupid. We are on our way," Cody said randomly. Josh looked around. It sounded like Cody was right beside him, but he was alone. "And what's the plan? We can't just walk in there like this and take the target out," Josh replied. "We have a plan, and we can see you on radar, so don't move. We'll be there soon," Cody said and continued.

"Wyatt is having some trouble with these zip line things, but we will be there soon. By the way, are you getting any interference on your scanner?" Cody asked, and Josh realized he had no idea what Cody was talking about.

"Let me check it," Josh replied and concentrated on the scanners. The computer responded as his whole vision changed into something that resembled thermal vision. The machine on the ground was glowing white-hot, and the people were visible, but something was making the sky seem to fade in and out from black to white and black again.

"Yeah, my scanner is freaking out about something too. I'm not sure if it's bad tech or what. Maybe Blake can solve this problem with one shot. The cops have the thing surrounded, and it's not moving anymore. I doubt it stays that way for long," Josh said and was fine with waiting for now as long as it wasn't moving.

## 14

Josh waited and watched the machine, but nothing changed when a voice came from behind him.

"Thanks for waiting. We didn't need any more attention," Cody said, and he turned to see the rest of them. He was glad to see them. He liked their suits, too. "Any ideas on what to do? The crowd isn't making this easy," Dustin asked as he looked over the edge to see the standoff. Blake looked at him.

"Hello, sniper rifle."

It was a typical Dustin quirk to miss the painfully obvious.

"Oh, right, duh," Dustin said and looked back to the crowd below. "Are you positive this guy is supposed to be on our team, and it's not some kind of mistake?" Wyatt asked. He sometimes found it hard to believe how clueless Dustin could be, and the commander sighed.

"Yeah, I'm amazed too," Cody said and turned to watch as Blake was taking aim. "Don't miss. Team, back off so people don't look in this direction and see a bunch of armored maniacs on a building. We really don't need that kind of attention," Cody said.

"We're just outside of the perimeter of the cops. Look to the buildings left and right, above the thing. They aren't paying attention to us, stay low, and it'll be fine," Blake said as he looked through the scope. The shot was easy enough, but he'd never had to do this before in front of so many people.

Blake pulled the trigger, and the shot fired without a single sound from his new rifle. The bullet hit the machine in the head, sparks and fire followed the shot, and it fell to its knees, then to the ground in less than a second. Blake backed off, and the scene below erupted with confusion.

"Yep, I can tell we were needed for this mission, armor and all. I mean, you'd think the world was coming to an end. Let's go home," Wyatt said in a sarcastic tone at the ease with which the robot was taken out.

Then, from above, a sound came. A high-pitched whistling sound filled the night sky, and Wyatt looked up to the sky then thinking he'd spoken far too soon. It was something falling at a high rate of speed.

"No. You don't think," Cody said and looked up into the night sky. His suspicions were confirmed. The others watched as flaming spheres lit up the sky as if the stars were beginning to fall. "Wyatt, you don't get to talk anymore. Everything you say backfires," Josh said as he gazed at the falling objects.

"Don't look at me. I was kidding," Wyatt replied. There was no time to laugh at Wyatt's remark as the things began to slam down into various places like meteorites, causing explosions and large jets of flame on impact, some far away and some far too close.

"Cody, we can't stay here. This is more serious than we thought," Blake said as he stood up, looking at the destruction around them. "Any ideas where they are coming from?" Dustin asked and brought up a good point. "The computer says they were fired from the ocean if the landing pattern holds up," Wyatt said and was hoping none of these falling things was going to fall on them.

"I know, but we will wait for the orders of the Syndicate," Cody said because he was sure they would pull through this time like they had every other time before. He wasn't sure how they missed an army of machines hiding in the ocean. It made no sense, but he was hoping that it soon would all be clear.

## 15

The city of Los Angeles, at least the city as far as they could tell from here, was under a full-scale invasion by what looked like machines. The artificial meteor shower didn't show any signs of slowing down.

"Oh man. Do you suppose this is it? The aliens are invading, and we are all doomed to be destroyed by aliens from another world. I always knew this would be how the world ended," Josh was in a rare panic all of a sudden. Dustin was going to say something to try and calm him down, but their proximity warnings went off.

One of the spheres landed on their rooftop and smashed through it, sending fire and debris in all directions. "Well, how about that, no one got crushed into paste. It can't be that bad of a day," Dustin said as the five of them approached the hole it made to see what was going to happen.

They watched as the monster broke out of its charred metal sphere and stood up, oblivious to the others. The same scene was playing out all around them, all over the city, at the exact same time, but at least the meteor shower had come to an end.

The human-shaped machine stood there, plated armor and

all. It looked like a knight and was as tall as any of them, but for now, it remained motionless. It was a different model than the one Blake had shot minutes earlier.

"Impressive-looking thing, but let's break it before it tries to kill us," Josh said as he backed off a step. "It's not aliens, but look at the insignia on the shoulder. It's a Z, as in Zeron Special Forces. It looks the same as it did two years ago," Cody said, trying to remember if he was right or not.

"I didn't know they were all killer robots. What gives?" Dustin asked, wanting to learn more about it. The eyes began to glow blue, and it was coming to life. Then it jumped out of the crater and landed on the opposite side from where they were. "That's nice and all, but can we break it now? I don't think it's friendly," Wyatt said, waiting for the order to attack this thing before it was too late. Cody nodded.

"Kill this thing. We'll get information from Blackfire later," Cody said, and Wyatt wasted no time in reacting. He ran and dashed through the air over the crater. At the same time, he swung his blade at the machine's neck as it was coming to life, and his blade carved through the steel, severing the head from the neck. Wyatt landed behind it.

Unexpectedly, blue fluid sprayed from the neck as it fell to the ground. Wyatt turned around. "Huh, I expected a little more fight," he said.

Cody looked around and saw the same scene happening all around them. These knights were coming to life. "Cody to Blackfire, come in, we have something of a situation here. We could use an update," Cody said.

"We are aware. We are trying to contact Zeron now, but treat them as hostile. We don't know what is going on or where they came from, but we'll figure it out soon. Until then, stand by and good luck," Heath said and cut off communication.

"Well. I guess we sit here and wait. Dustin, figure out what this thing is. Blake, keep an eye on what they are doing. If they attack anyone, consider it an attack on us and act accordingly. Wyatt, Josh, and I will make sure that nothing comes crawling up the sides and gives us a nasty surprise," Cody said and walked to the edge and looked down. He had no idea what he was looking at, but due to the reactions of the people below, none of it was good.

# 16

"Erin, call Zeron Island. We need to know what the deal is," Heath said. Erin was already on the job. "You think so? I am contacting them, but no one is picking up. I'm not sure what else you want me to do," she replied, pushing the green button again to send the signal. Erin looked over at the woman she had pushed out of the way in frustration.

"Sorry," she said. The blonde shrugged, having no idea what to say. "Thought I could push the button better than you do. I guess you do a fine job, too," Erin said. The communications officer was about to respond when the signal connected with a harsh beep.

Erin didn't bother waiting to be told about putting the call through to the main screen.

"What the hell is going on? Why are you attacking Los Angeles? Did someone pay you a mountain of gold?" Heath asked, but the screen was black. Whoever was on the other end wasn't eager to be seen.

"Attacking? We aren't attacking anything. You've got it wrong," a man said from the black with a raspy cough. "The hell you're not. We are seeing—"Heath was cut off by the voice in the dark.

"It all went wrong. Project Dead Steel didn't work as we planned. It was perfect," the man struggled to say this. It was obvious he was injured. "You've got to tell me more," Heath said, becoming worried about what was coming next.

"Dead Steel went rogue. We wanted to make the perfect weapon, the perfect cyborg. Dead Steel worked, but the counterpart---" The connection phased out for a second. "Files are ready for transfer. You want them? Not like they'll do you any good. Sorry about all of this," the man said. The communication with the island died, maybe the messenger too.

"We have files, Project Dead Steel and Silver Queen from the looks of it," Erin said as she began looking through them.

"Only the important stuff, Erin," Heath said, and Erin looked up and couldn't believe what she had read. "We need to isolate that whole city now. Call the President, call whomever you need to call, because if we don't stop this right now—" she trailed off then as she kept reading. "Erin, tell me what is going on." Heath was trying to keep calm, but she wasn't making it easy.

"The machines, Dead Steel seems to be stable, but the rest of them are infectious. It's unlike anything I've ever seen. Zeron science tried to create organic metal, and they succeeded. Heath, there are hundreds of pages here. Long story short, we can't allow this to spread any farther than where it is right now. In the meantime, I will find out how to detect this stuff so we can destroy it. Get everyone on this," she said, giving the orders without even thinking about it.

Heath looked at the black screen and made a choice. He decided that Erin was right.

"Alright, I will get Emily and the others working on this problem too. We need to know what we are dealing with," Heath said and walked away and moved to his office.

He sat down and picked up the red phone on his desk. It only dialed to two places: the Syndicate High Council and the White House, and right now he needed to talk to the President.

The White House became aware of the attack and the strange declaration of war that was given by someone that looked to be in body armor like everyone else, but other than that, everyone was clueless as to what was going on.

"There were no threats, nothing like this. No listening post anywhere in the world picked up on it," McRaven said as they watched the video again.

"Tell me this robot-looking thing didn't get its war message out on national television. The last thing we need is a panic across the country," President August said. He ran his hand through his silver hair in disbelief. First this Cyranthis insanity, now this? There was no way he'd be reelected. Not unless he could handle this mess, the faster the better.

"No, it was just a local news channel, but panic is spreading through the city. We've already blocked the internet providers from outside access," someone else said. He stared at the machine as the voices in the room started to get louder with suggestions on what to do next and how. Each official was infected with a fear against an enemy none of them had seen.

The President was distracted. Something at his side was buzzing, and there was only one person who he knew could be on the other end. He took the black cell phone off his belt, and as he did, the room grew quiet. The highest-ranking officials saw this and wondered who could be calling at a time like this. The President raised his hand, and everybody in the room shut up.

"Hello," he said. They waited to see what was coming next. "Are you sure?" he asked after a few seconds of silence. "Yes, I understand. Just make sure to do your part. Don't screw this up," he said and paused, wincing a little bit, as if someone on the other end didn't like his tone.

"Already there? Good, we'll be there too," he replied and hung up the phone.

"California declared a code Delta Green. A biological attack of unknown origin has been detected in Los Angeles, and it is highly infectious and lethal. I am sending the military in to quarantine the city until the threat has been dealt with," the others wondered how the information could have come that fast.

"I am declaring martial law in that city until further notice, and all surrounding areas. You know what to do, so get to work. I will be announcing it soon. Shut everything down in and around the city as fast as you can. Put everyone in the city on high alert. This is a level four threat," August said, and the officials were surprised, but now that they had direction, they got to work, leaving the Oval Office. McRaven stayed behind.

"Was it him?" he asked in a hushed tone. "It was," August replied. "God help us all," he finished, but now was no time to give in to fear. "Set up the studio. I need to get on camera now," the President finished. McRaven didn't bother to ask more questions. "Yes, sir," he replied and left the office.

President August didn't have time to look good for the camera. In ten minutes, he found himself sitting in front of a camera, no teleprompter, no script or time to think about what he was going to say first. The red light on the camera turned on.

"My fellow Americans. Minutes ago, the city of Los Angeles was the target of a biological terrorist attack. Information at this time is limited. As of right now, I am mobilizing the military to seal off the city. If you live in Los Angeles and the greater area, do not attempt to leave. You will be shot. Stay in your homes and seal them as best as you can. Find shelter now and remain there until further notice. Looters will be shot on sight. This is a civil emergency," he said with a hard look into the camera.

"I repeat. Martial law has been declared for all of Los Angeles and the surrounding areas until the threat has been dealt with. The military has full authority to use deadly force or arrest anyone they find on the streets. Do not go to work. Do not go to the store for supplies. If you are on the road, go home now. If you are out of the city, stay where you are. All flights are being diverted. If you are in the city, do not panic and once again, stay home. This is a time of crisis, but only if we work together will we prevail. This too will pass. Good luck and good night," he said and wanted to add "may God have mercy on your souls," but decided that might be too grim.

The little red light went off. "Make sure that message repeats on all the local networks," he said, knowing it was impossible to keep this information hidden for long. The man behind the camera nodded, and the crew started packing up.

It was a short and simple message, but its words were straight to the point. He had no doubt that this would not go over well with anyone, and not even he knew what the true nature of the threat was. All of this was making him feel nervous.

# 17

Heath and the others were watching. Once the announcement was made, they knew the Squad had full authority to do what needed to be done.

"General, the guys are waiting for the order. We're wasting time here," Erin said and waited for him to do something. "Heath?" Erin asked as she turned around. Heath nodded. "Do it," he replied.

Erin knew what needed to be done and turned back to the communications panel. "Cody, listen, the machines need to be destroyed. Zeron forces have been corrupted by something called Project Dead Steel. Martial law was declared, and the military is mobilizing to quarantine the city. Cody, you've got to destroy all those machines. Don't let any escape. I'll be sending you an update soon," Erin said.

"I want a full report on these machines within the hour. I need to report to the high council, but I think they, as usual, know more than I do already," Heath said, turned around, and left.

"Patch me into the advance recon cameras. I want to see what's going on," Erin said. The main screen in front of them turned from black to a view from a helicopter, but from here the city looked as if there was nothing wrong with it. All the lights on the skyscrapers and on the ground made it look normal.

"Approaching green zone and all seems to be fine. They couldn't have picked a better time to attack. The blockades are going up and traffic is coming to a halt. All plans are going well so far," someone said from behind the camera. "I can't believe something like this is happening. Bioweapons are my worst nightmare. I'm glad we have these hazmat suits," someone else replied behind the camera.

Erin couldn't help but feel sorry for them. With the little information she had, she knew those suits would do no good. The only thing that could help them now would be a gun and some quick thinking.

# 18

Cody got the order, but it was difficult to hear over Dustin's constant pleading for attention at the same time.

"Cody, you need to see this, right now!" Dustin was excited about something, but he sounded a little bit scared too. "What is it? Calm down already. I'm coming," Cody said, wondering what could be so important as he made his way around the crater.

"Watch this," Dustin said and put the head of the machine close to the body. The wires began to reach out towards one another. "What?" Cody asked, tilting his head a little.

"A repair function of some kind. I don't understand it, but these things are more than just machines," Dustin said, and Cody watched as the head was trying to reunite with the body.

"Orders came in to wreck all of these things. Now I see why," Cody said.

"The first one I killed didn't have a recovery system. The body is still there," Blake said. It was an interesting point, but Cody didn't care.

"Doesn't matter. They want them all destroyed. We do it," Cody said and took a step back, as did the others. He pulled out his plasma cannon that was at his side and fired.

The metal skin burned and melted into nothing before their eyes, and the bright blue beam of plasma was so hot that it melted through the roof into the floors below.

"Cody, what the hell were you thinking? There might be people in there, and you just destabilized the whole building," Blake said as the intense glow faded away. "Not to mention you gave away our position to the entire city," Wyatt added, not expecting Cody to blast a hole through a building.

Cody himself was shocked at the sheer power of his weapon and had nothing to say to defend his to work," Cody said but never took his eyes off the hole he made and wondered if there was anyone down there. "I'd never shot a plasma cannon before. I didn't know it was going to do that. We need to get to work."

The alarm was going off, but he didn't hear any screaming, so that was a good sign. Or everyone was dead. It wasn't their problem.

The five of them turned to face the rising smoke and flames in the distance of the night. Dustin looked at the growing chaos, and a thought occurred as he took it all in. "Do you suppose it's real? The whole end-of-the-world thing on the twenty-first of this year?" Dustin asked.

"Maybe, but it's only the 19th. I think we have some room to stop it once we figure out what it is and how to do it without burning down the city," Cody said as he put his cannon away. "You know, some people think the date is wrong and the beginning of the end of the world ends around 2020 instead," Wyatt replied.

Josh laughed. "What's so funny?" Blake asked. "Wyatt thinks the human race is going to make it that long," Josh replied. "It won't if we just stand here and watch," Blake replied.

"Right, Blake has a point. If we keep standing here, everything is going to fall apart. Let's get out of here and see what we can see," Wyatt said and looked over the edge. There was nothing down there but broken metal shells and craters. All the machines had left. "That's an ambush waiting to happen," Blake said.

"Yeah, we need a better vantage point," Cody replied and looked across the way. "We'll stick to the rooftops until we come up with a plan," he said and pointed across the road to another building.

"We'll go to the next roof, to a building that isn't on fire, and make our way down to the street to get a closer look. Maybe this time you don't have to show the whole world where we are?" Wyatt asked as he glared at Cody.

"Yeah, don't look at me with that tone. I'll reach through that helmet and tear your eyes out," Cody replied. "Noted," Wyatt replied, knowing he'd do his best to try it.

The five of them looked to the nearest building and backed up as far as they could. "So, this is going to work, right?" Josh asked. "Yeah, timing is a bit tricky, but it should work. The computer will help out too," Dustin replied.

"Never needed to trust a computer before," Blake said, looking at the ledge they were all going to jump from. "Things change, I guess," Josh replied.

"Alright, shut up and start running," Cody said and took off. The others did as well. Wyatt pulled ahead and was the first to jump. The second he did, he felt like he was flying. It didn't last long. At the highest point of the leap, the marker on his display turned green, and he fired the line.

It fired, and the end impaled itself in the wall. At once, the line reeled him to where he needed to be. Three other ziplines did the same.

Dustin's line fired as it was meant to, however, it plowed through a window and hooked on the corner. The second the line began to retract. Dustin's line bent and sent him swinging around wildly to the other side of the building.

"Son of a Q!" Dustin said as he slammed into the wall. Whatever his line had hooked on broke, and he was in free fall. Dustin hit the ground. Everything on the inside of his armor went black, but only for a few seconds as the suit started to turn back on.

"I'm not broken. Imagine that," he said and was surprised that the armor didn't break into pieces. But now he could hear voices in the distance and wondered if people had seen him fall. He sat up and looked towards the voices and realized that it wasn't him anyone was talking about.

Dustin saw the machines surrounding the first responders to the disaster, and now he could see something else had fallen with the invaders. To him, it looked like a metal shed, and he had no idea what it was for.

Most of Dustin's mind wanted him to jump up and stop whatever event was about to happen, yet another small part needed to know what was going to happen next.

"Guys, I am patching you through to see what I see. I think this is something we need to know," Dustin said to them and synched up his visuals with theirs.

"Also, Dustin, you need to learn how to aim that zip line. I've got to say I haven't laughed that hard in a long time," Josh replied. Dustin ignored it as he watched one of the bigger machines walk towards a member of the SWAT team, who in turn opened fire on them, but the bullets did nothing but bounce off. Another machine to the left let loose a green energy pulse from its eyes that knocked everyone down. Dustin could still see their life signs.

The first one grabbed its intended target by the neck with its right hand and picked the man up with ease. Without saying a thing, it walked to the building, and the door opened automatically. The man was tossed into the black as if he were a toy. The door slid shut behind him.

Less than fifteen seconds passed when the SWAT member came walking out the other side, but he looked like the first one, a man half covered in steel plating, flesh mixed with metal.

Dustin watched as the new soldier walked to the now recovering, but terrified, group of people, lifted its left arm, and fired.

Thin metal lines came from the top of the wrist and hit everyone. Dustin counted twenty people, and they started to have seizures.

"Processing time one hour. Expansion protocol active. No life forms detected in the immediate area. Seek them out," the machine said to the other. Then both walked in opposite directions.

"Guys, this is happening all over the city. Got a plan?" Dustin asked as he stood up and armed his weapons but stopped as soon as he saw the victims starting to move and retreated into the shadows where he fell.

From here, he could already see the metal tearing out of the flesh and the people. They were all screaming, still awake. The estimated processing time of an hour was a bad estimate. It was going to happen a lot faster.

19

"Cody, we need to stop this," Wyatt said as he watched, realizing that this was going to turn out to be a world-ending threat.

"Don't you think I know that? The only way we can do it is by splitting up and making sure we can take these things out so that there is nothing left. Do it right the first time," Cody replied.

"This is the plot of *Unicorn Hunter X: Robohorn*," Blake said as it hit him, and no one else had any clue what he was talking about.

"The X Series movie where people tried to create a unicorn killer out of Uni-DNA and mix it with a machine and it worked, but the DNA was too strong and the thing used its magic to replicate itself out of people and unicorn alike, resulting in a rare alliance between the two to eradicate a common enemy. The plot was not original. It came from an arc of episodes from *Star Traveler: The Lost Adventures*, where a machine race sought to take over the alliance by turning everything into machines like they were, and that was stolen by an even older show called *Time Doctor* in the sixties about—" Blake was ranting, and Wyatt cut him off.

"Dude, back to reality. So, a mad scientist was influenced by some television show, but we need to come up with a plan of attack to end this," Wyatt said and thought about calling him something else, but it wasn't worth it.

"I am back to reality. I am just saying how similar this is to things I've seen before," Blake said and looked down at the scene below. The television show looked fake at least. This was horrible.

"It seems like Dustin has something of a plan going on down there at least," Blake said as he looked down off the side of the building. The others turned to look at him too. "What is he doing down there?" Cody asked, confused.

"You could ask him, but somehow I don't think that would explain much," Josh said. He was sure that Dustin was insane because of all the things he did on a regular basis.

Dustin watched the people jerk and slowly come to life and knew that he needed to do something about this. It was a techno-organic virus, and it needed to be wiped out. The victims were still alive, writhing in pain. They were in front of an office building, at least it looked like one.

Dustin always wanted to do this to an office building. It looked like an office building anyway, and activated his wrist-mounted flamethrowers. "Death to the cubicle," he said.

"What in the hell are you doing?" Cody screamed at Dustin and was prepared to stop him as his hand moved back to his cannon. He didn't want to use it on a friend.

"I have an idea, watch and see," Dustin said as he let his fire loose onto the structure. The white flames tore through the front windows, and the building caught fire. The whole process only took a few seconds and looked like an explosion.

Dustin was sure they wouldn't detect him. The infected people got to their feet and took notice of the fire.

"Heat source is detected, threat assessment medium. Investigation of area is commencing," one of them said in a mechanical voice, and the group of machines started to walk toward the growing fire.

Dustin raised his arms and prepared to shoot all of them at once while they were still in a group and would make easy targets.

"Hey, those machines are people. We can't just break them and be done with it. There's got to be a way to reverse the process," Cody said, realizing what the outcome was going to be.

"Screw it, this is war and they need to die. There isn't any hope for them, and if we waste time, it won't make a difference what we do anyway." Josh was with Dustin on this one and decided to go help him kill them all and leapt off the building. Blake was confused.

"Guys, I have a rifle that could—oh, never mind. Just run off into battle, yeah. That makes sense. Sure, I could kill them from here, but where's the fun in that?" Blake asked himself and watched the others rush into battle. He wondered why he even bothered to show up.

"Don't worry about me. I'll be fine up here, alone," he said to them as he put his rifle on the ledge and watched them go do whatever it was they were planning to do.

## 20

Josh didn't care that these machines were people a few minutes ago. This was a threat to everyone. He wanted his revenge from before. He landed on the ground behind the one at the back of the group and grabbed it by its left shoulder and spun it around to face him. It was a face twisted with pain and fear, strands of silver growing through the flesh, pulsating.

Josh didn't hesitate, and with the other hand, he punched the thing right in the face to send it flying into the flaming building along with the one in front of it at the same time. This time, the advantage was his, and he was a bit shocked how strong this armor was. He couldn't believe what he did.

"Well, so much for the element of surprise, you idiot. Do you think you could be any less obvious? I had it under control," Dustin said and switched to his minigun and started shooting into the enemy. He managed to shred another two of them to pieces, sending blood and steel towards the fire, but the chance to take them all down at once was gone.

The rest of them avoided the attack by scattering out of the way, moving like broken dolls.

"Damn it, Josh, I hate you sometimes," Dustin said as they

got out of the way. "Don't hate me because you can't aim worth a damn. That's your problem, not mine," Josh replied and almost laughed but would never admit that he screwed this plan up, at least not to Dustin.

"Let me show you how it's done," Wyatt said and, like Josh before him, attacked the enemy head-on. He attacked the one in the center, closest to the growing inferno behind it.

He was filled with confidence as he swung his blade with what he figured was his full speed and strength at this person's metal-covered neck. The blade hit the neck and stopped on impact.

"Oh crap," was all Wyatt had time to say as the enemy reached up with its cold, metal-covered left hand and with the right, it clenched its fist and swung. The impact to his face was stronger than he thought it would be. Wyatt and the blade he refused to drop went flying.

Wyatt slammed into the commander, the two of them were knocked to the ground and slid against the road until they were stopped by a police car that still had its lights flashing. "Wyatt, you suck at this," Cody said and pushed him off.

"Sorry, how was I supposed to know my armor sucks? I didn't get to test it, you know?" Wyatt asked and stood up along with Cody. As the commander stood up, he decided this needed to come to an end.

"Stand back, I got this," Cody said and drew his weapon, set it to a wide angle, and took aim as the others made sure they were behind that cannon. The metal-infested enemy didn't detect a threat and shambled in the direction of the commander in order to attack.

Cody couldn't help but think that the fading humanity in their wrecked bodies was doing its best to try and slow them down. "May God forgive me," he said.

Cody pulled the trigger, and the brilliant blue wave of death screamed from the end of that cannon. The machines could only watch for a second as it came. Their beady red eyes widened for a split second. Then it crashed into them, melting the organic parts and the steel parts alike into a pile of black, misshapen puddles with pairs of legs and misshapen arms sticking out as the beam melted everything.

The nameless building behind where the monsters stood had a massive hole in it now. Smoke poured out of the opening, and fire came from the windows above it. The place was ready to collapse. Something was outlined against the flames. One lone, blackened metallic figure was moving towards them, smoke rolled off its body.

Cody turned to shoot the last one, but before he could, its head was torn off in an instant and it fell to its knees, black blood pouring from the wound. The four of them looked towards Blake. He was standing there on the roof, pointing at his sniper rifle, then giving a thumbs up. They were sure he was smiling under that helmet as he was doing it.

The original two machines marched back at the sudden violence. The squad got ready to fight.

"Target obtained. Designate: Syndicate Tech. Mission: Destroy," they said in an electronically altered voice in unison before they dropped dead. Wyatt and Cody looked at one another and didn't quite know what this meant.

Dustin looked at Josh. "Really hate you sometimes," he said, thinking all of this could have been avoided if he had gotten them all at once.

"Yeah, so everyone keeps telling me. I'm used to it," Josh replied and put his weapon away.

"So, is that all of them?" Dustin asked as he looked at the mess that didn't need to be made.

"Looks like it, but still, now I get why they are calling it a biological attack. This is a nightmare," Wyatt said and couldn't help but feel sorry for the victims, but it was obvious they had no other choice than to kill them all.

"So, we can assume that those last two alerted every enemy

in range that we are a threat and this tactic won't work again. We will need to be more careful from here on out," Cody said, and as he said it, the effect of martial law kicked in as the loud klaxon air raid sirens began to cut through the night air.

"Now it's a party," Josh said as the eerie sound echoed in all directions.

## 21

The sound of the military jets crossing over the night skies and the sounds of helicopters echoing as well in the night were coming from every direction.

The city would soon be cut off from the rest of the world and in the control of the military to isolate the threat. Cody couldn't help but wonder if they weren't going to make things worse. More warm bodies to convert into iron things. There was no time to think about it now.

"We can't stay here. Dustin, take out that machine shed and let's move," Cody said and turned to look at it, but Dustin had made his way over to it and was already studying it.

"Do you know what this is, or looks like to me? This is an organic converter of some kind, it turns people into them!" The squad was speechless at his firm grasp of the obvious, but it was as if there was something else he was trying to say but couldn't find the words.

"Yes, we all saw what it does. Do you think you could break it now instead of telling us what we already know?" Josh said. He was annoyed with Dustin and wanted to punch him, but he resisted the urge.

"You don't understand. Let me check something," he said.

Dustin moved to the side of the thing and tore open the side of the silver container and exposed the wires. He crossed a few of them together carefully. He thought he knew what he was doing, but whatever he did didn't work. With a violent spark, the whole thing exploded in a ball of green fire. The force of the explosion sent him back a few feet through the air, and he landed on his back on the pavement.

"Ouch," Dustin said as he got up from the ground, acting as if nothing had happened. Cody was left speechless. "What was that all about?" Wyatt asked.

"Nothing, just a stupid idea," Dustin replied.

"So, Commander, what is the plan for this mission? How are we going to avoid everyone?" Blake asked as they walked away.

"I don't know. We're supposed to kill all these things and go home," Cody said, and Dustin joined in.

"That's not going to be possible. These things can replicate, and their numbers will become more than we can handle, millions in hours I predict," Dustin said, once again saying something they all knew already.

"I swear I'm going to punch him," Josh mumbled.

"Wait, these things wanted to declare war against the Cyranthis religion. Whoever is responsible for this mess will be attacking the churches. The next biggest one is downtown, and I think we'll find the source of this disaster there. It's a good place to start," Josh said, and it was as good a plan as any.

"Downtown is far from here. We'll need to move fast. Blake and Wyatt, scout ahead and find us a clear path. Rooftops, side streets—I don't care how you do it. We'll be right behind you," Cody said, and the two of them, without another word, took off running into the dark.

In the distance, the sound of gunfire could be heard. The military or someone was already engaging the enemy. "We'll find the source of this infection and take it out," Cody said.

"What if that isn't enough? We don't have any guarantee that this will do anything, or even if it's there," Dustin said and had a point.

"We'll deal with it when that happens. Until then, think positive for a while. It's good for you. Now let's get out of here before someone sees us and thinks we're machines, too," Cody said, and they followed Blake and Wyatt.

## 22

Blake and Wyatt were quick to take to the rooftops and stick to the shadows. It only took a few seconds of looking around to see that the way through was going to be anything but easy. Mobs of people in a panic. It appeared as if the entire city had disobeyed the orders and came out to panic together.

"Suggestions, navigator?" Wyatt asked Blake, who was still looking around.

"Downtown is still far away, but there has to be an easier route than jumping," Blake said but didn't see any useful options.

"That wasn't the suggestion I was hoping for, but what do you suppose that is?" Wyatt pointed down, and Blake couldn't believe he missed it, but maybe it was selective blindness.

"You think we can just—well, why is there just a train sitting there at the station?" Blake asked.

"Martial law, genius," Wyatt replied. Of course, there was a mob of people demanding to get on the train, but the police weren't letting anyone through.

"So, do we just take it or what?" Wyatt asked.

"I don't know, but if we want to get there fast, this is our best shot," Blake said and tried to decide how to do it, but nothing sane was coming to mind.

"Cody, we found a way there, but there is a bit of an issue. You're the commander, so do some commanding or whatever. We'll wait here," Blake said through the intercom.

"We're on our way. Be there in a few minutes," Cody replied.

"Do you think we'll actually save anyone this time? I mean this is insane. Who'd do something like this?" Wyatt asked, then as he looked down at the people on the ground, desperate to get out even if it meant going into danger to get to anywhere safe.

"I don't know. Crazy is kind of what we do, so it could go either way," Blake said and watched for any unwanted surprises. The city was crawling with threats by now, and with a crowd like this, there were sure to be some on the way.

It was only minutes before the other three made it to the roof and walked to the edge. There were the people—that was the problem. Cody already had a plan in mind. It was going to be complicated.

"Yep, that'll do," the commander said and continued. "Alright, we need to move fast. Blake, do you think you can get to the front unseen? Once you do that, the rest of us will be in place. All you have to do is get the train rolling, and as soon as you do, we'll jump on from over there and—" Cody was cut off when Dustin slammed his weapon into Josh's back and sent him for a thirty-foot fall off the roof.

"They have never seen us before. They'll think we are the bad guys. Sorry, but your plan was getting on my nerves, and we just don't have the time," Dustin said and jumped off the side without another word.

"Or we can just be stupid about it. His plans are about as thought out as yours usually are, Wyatt," Cody said as he watched them do whatever it was Dustin had planned. Fighting the police wasn't part of his plan now, or ever. It was too late that Cody and Blake saw military units pulling up to help take care of the situation.

"My plans are good sometimes, shut up," Wyatt replied as they watched the Army arrive.

"So, we're fighting the army now too? We might as well just take on everyone at the same time. What could go wrong?" Cody asked. In his mind, all he could see was an incoming disaster.

## 23

The green Jeeps pulled up outside the crowd, and the soldiers got out. A man in the lead Jeep cracked his neck as he got out. He'd waited for something like this his whole life and gave a nod to the soldier in the passenger side, who flipped a switch.

"Ladies and Gentlemen. This is the United States Army. If you do not disperse and return to your homes at once, you will be shot. There will be no more warnings. Martial law is in effect as of twenty minutes ago," Will said through the mounted megaphone.

The crowd turned. "You can't kill us all," someone yelled out. "Fascist scum," another cried, and the crowd turned its rage on the Army. Will smiled. "Enemies, foreign and domestic," he said with a slight smile and lifted his arm. The soldiers aimed their weapons at the crowd and almost gave the order to fire when two heavy somethings landed behind them beyond the streetlights. Will looked up. The crowd grew silent too.

"Sir, two of them have just landed behind us! Orders, Captain?" one of the men shouted as he got out of the Jeep. Will turned around to see. Will took a good look at the things coming toward the crowd and noted that they looked different than the first ones they met, but he didn't care.

"Alright, take these two down, I'll get all the civvies on the ground. I'm not responsible for morons who stand in the way of a bullet," Will ordered and drew his weapon.

"Listen up. Hostiles are coming this way, and we will be shooting. If you don't wish to get shot, lay flat on the ground now or run and cover your ears," Will said through his loudspeaker to the mass of people. He didn't have time to worry about them. The crowd panicked and started to get down.

"Open fire," Will yelled as if it were an afterthought. Two fifty-caliber machine guns attached to the larger armored vehicles did that. The roar of the cannons obliterated the sound of the panic, the sound of anything else.

"You know, my only regret is that I can't hate you more than I already do," Josh said to Dustin as he dived out of the way the second the cannon opened fire. The armor was tough, but Josh was smart enough to try and avoid any damage he didn't need to take.

Dustin, on the other hand, lifted his arms and returned fire with his wrist-mounted miniguns into the troops and the crowd. Josh watched in disbelief at what he was seeing.

"You think you got some firepower? Wait until you get a taste of this," he yelled as the fifty-caliber bullets slammed into Dustin and bounced off his orange armor.

Dustin's fire destroyed two Jeeps at once. The bullets shredded through their armor at such a rapid pace they exploded. The people manning the guns were killed. Dustin laughed at the flames, the death, and all the carnage.

Josh thought he could hear laughing and he could see he was killing people. It didn't look like he was going to stop at the soldiers either.

Josh got back up, rushed to Dustin's side, and pulled his arms into the sky, stopping the attack. "What in the hell are you doing!" Josh screamed at him, as Dustin stopped shooting. The men on the machine guns were dead, burning. The crowd had injuries, and the other soldiers did too.

Blood was all over the ground, the walls of the train too. It was a distraction, but of the worst kind. Josh looked at the carnage and had no words for it. No time for remorse or stopping now.

"Damn it man, get on the train," Josh said, and Dustin snapped out of the madness.

In the chaos, the other three had managed to get onto the train and get it moving. Josh and Dustin got onto the train as it pulled away.

Cody was quick to meet Dustin and throw him to the train floor. "Give me one reason why I don't shoot you right now," he said and pulled out his plasma cannon, putting it to Dustin's face. "Commander, how good would it have looked if the big bad machine invaders didn't shoot back? This is war, and in war, people die," Dustin said as he lay there. Cody figured he had a point, as horrible as it was.

"If you need another reason, I wouldn't recommend shooting your plasma cannon on a train. It might be worse than you expect," Dustin said, and Cody held the cannon on him for a few seconds more before putting it away.

"We need to get off this train before we get to the end of the tracks. It will be tracked, and at the other end, there will be people waiting for us," Wyatt said, trying to break the tension. He was still in shock about what Dustin did and didn't know what to think about it.

"Agreed, we'll jump off as close as we can get." Cody said, but didn't take his eyes off Dustin. "If you ever pull that again, it will be your last time," Cody said and turned around.

"We'll see, commander," Dustin replied. He hated war, but when it came down to getting something done, he wasn't afraid to do what was necessary.

The others looked out the windows, none of them knowing

what to say right now, trying to get the sight of all that blood out of their minds, preparing for whatever came next.

## 24

The Squad didn't know it, but everything they were doing was being recorded the second the weapons were activated. They were all quite horrified at what they were seeing back on Blackfire Island.

"I told you the armors were a bad idea. Anything based on the designs of a Zodiac member who was insane to begin with is a terrible idea. The armor sickness is already getting to Dustin. He is killing Americans. You saw it, it's all turning out like I said it would," Emily said to Erin and Heath.

She never liked the idea of using armor for the next step of the Squad to begin with, and every argument she ever had against it was coming true. The evidence was apparent now, but there was nothing any of them could do.

"We have to trust them. There isn't much we can do. The Council wanted this. If it gets too bad, we can send in the other team we have on standby to take the Squad down," Heath said to try and calm Emily down. She couldn't even look at the screen or either of them right now.

"Them? No, we can't possibly send them into the field," Erin said. She knew that the Chemical Dragon unit was nowhere near good enough to do the job.

"The Squad is on their own," she added and prayed that they wouldn't kill anyone else. It was all she could do and hope someone was listening.

"On another interesting note, I can't contact them. Something is jamming the communications. The real-time feed is still alright, but everything else is being blocked, and if it can block us, something bigger is involved," Heath said, trying to change the subject and continued. "Go get Nick and Roger on this problem as soon as you can. I'm sure they're in the lab," he said.

Emily got the message. She didn't want to watch anymore of the Squad's brutality in first person view no less. "I'll go find them," Emily said and left the command center. Erin waited until the door slid shut.

"Really, Heath? Dustin just opens up on a crowd, kills people, and the best you can come up with is we'll just have to trust them?" Erin was disappointed. "Yeah, what choice do we have? Do you want to go down there and give them a lecture? What else can we do?" he replied. "I don't like the way this is turning out either, but if they get the job done and stop a plague of living metal, it's worth it," he replied. Erin hated that, but couldn't help but agree, at least for now. "Fine," she said. "Can we download stuff to their armor?" Erin asked.

"I think so, why?" Heath asked. "Because I think I found a way to track the metal," she replied.

## 25

The Blue Line train was three cars long, but that was two, too many. "Trains suck when it comes to going fast. Wyatt, could you just disconnect the last two cars so we can get this show on the road?" Blake said. He wanted to go as far as they could before they had to jump off, but it would take hours at this rate.

Wyatt sighed in frustration, feeling like nothing more than an errand boy so far. "Sure, I'll do that, Blake. I know how hard it is to keep the train on the tracks and going in a straight line at the same time," he said as he turned to walk away and towards the connecting points of the train in the back. It didn't take him long to get outside. "Did anyone even ask if I knew how?" he said as he got there, opening the door.

As he was going to sever the connection, he heard a strange buzzing coming from the sky that was getting louder than the sound of the train.

"I wonder what kind of nightmare this is going to be?" Wyatt asked with a great deal of sarcasm and looked up into the orange-tinted night sky. The night hid them but Wyatt's armor was able to detect something.

They were arrow shaped wings with a reflective surface to

keep them hidden. "What is up with all the machine things? Was there a sale at the tech store I didn't know about or what?" Wyatt said as he cut the link between the trains with one swing of his blade and then jumped to the top of the train once there was room.

"Guys, we have, uh, flying things coming for us. It seems like the machines want a little payback," Wyatt said into the intercom as he saw three of the winged things dive out of the sky and use thin green laser beams to tear the two train cars into flaming piles of junk in seconds.

"And what's the deal with all of these monsters and their lasers?" Cody asked as he pulled himself to the top of the train beside Wyatt. "No idea, but let's take them out before they decide to get serious. Squad, get into defensive positions. Don't let them pass and take out the rails ahead of the train. Blake, push this thing as fast as it'll go. We can't stay here," Cody said.

Wyatt took the hint and removed himself from the back of the train.

Josh stood on the back of the train car in the open door. He could see the enemies in the sky and knew that they were going to be hard to hit, but he opened fire on the flying ones, lifted his wrists, and opened fire into the sky but hit nothing as the small drones evaded the bullets. "Guys, this could require some teamwork," Josh said. "You don't say?" Cody replied.

Dustin and Cody wasted no time in taking aim and fired bullets and plasma energy into the sky. These things were too fast and spun through the air, mocking them.

Wyatt almost laughed as he watched from the front of the train. So far, the drones didn't shoot back, and he didn't understand why. Maybe they were tracking them, he wasn't sure.

"Nice going there, guys. Way to shoot the air like that," he looked at his blade and knew it would be as useless.

"Hey, I'll be right back," Wyatt said, but no one listened. He cut a hole in the roof and dropped inside. "Blake, give me your weapon," he said. "No," Blake replied. "You're not using it, and I think I could," he replied. "Damn it," he said, and the compartment opened. "Just don't wreck the thing," Blake said, preparing for an emergency stop if it was needed.

"Thanks," Wyatt said as he pulled himself to the top of the train. Blake didn't trust Wyatt, but right now he was still in the process of trying to figure out how to make this thing go faster without killing them. He wasn't a train operator, after all.

"Alright, fly boys. Let's see how you deal with this," Wyatt took aim and fired the rifle without bracing himself first. He never did find out if he hit one of the things or not because the recoil of the shot knocked him off his feet and over the side. He grabbed onto the edge and held on at the last second with his left hand, the right still held onto the rifle.

Blake winced as he heard the blast and watched Wyatt pull himself up from the brink of death from the front window of the train. "Yeah, he's gonna wreck it, idiot," Blake prepared for the worst.

"Alright, the second time should do it. No mistakes this time." He stood up and took aim again only to be taken by surprise, blindsided from the left. Wyatt needed to act fast, and he threw the rifle as soon as he was hit, hoping someone would catch it before it hit the ground. "Catch," he managed to yell.

The thing sprouted thin, yet strong arms ending in three claws and snatched Wyatt while he was distracted, and in seconds Wyatt and the flying thing were high in the air. Wyatt, for a brief second, didn't even know what was going on.

The armor could do many things, flying was not one of them.

"Why me?" Wyatt asked as he twisted his left wrist in the grip of the flying thing. The claws broke open, and sparks flew from them. The left hand let go. Wyatt used this chance to draw his sword and cut through the middle with ease.

"Ha, I win this round," he said as the two halves of the machine fell away from him, and now he was in a free fall but knew there was nothing he could do about it. "Gravity sucks," he said.

## 26

They watched as he fell to the ground somewhere in the distance, disappearing. "He can take care of himself, let's finish this," Cody said as the other drones began shooting back with their thin green beams, but because the cover fire from the squad was so good, they couldn't get a direct shot in.

The flying wings stopped flying chaotically and took a V formation in the sky and dropped back out of range. "They must be coming in for the kill. I think now would be a good time to find better ground to fight," Cody said, and Dustin agreed.

They began to move back towards the front of the speeding train. Josh didn't move from his spot. Even though he knew this was a bad idea. However, now that they were in a new formation, they would be easier to shoot down, but timing was everything.

They didn't know how dangerous those lasers were to their armor, but no one wanted to find out the hard way. Josh took aim.

"Josh, move!" Dustin yelled seconds too late as one of the man-sized winged things flew from the left side out of the dark.

Josh had no time to brace himself as the thing attempted to take him off the train. Instead, it was stopped. Josh grabbed and forced it to the ground and put his foot on the drone's underside. Those claws extended and flailed wildly, trying to defend itself.

Not wasting any time, Josh gripped its left arm and pulled it free from the body, creating a shower of red sparks as he did. Josh tossed the scrap metal off to the side, then he punched it straight through the middle. A spout of red flame came from the damage, but it was finally dead.

The whole ordeal took a few seconds. He turned to look at the ones still in the air as he picked up the one, he killed and threw it. The three in the air didn't notice anything was coming and didn't move. The wing in the middle was hit and exploded in midair, sending red fire trailing behind it. It reminded them of fireworks.

"Interesting development," Josh said as he watched this happen and now understood that they didn't or couldn't see their own kind as a threat.

"Just two left. Do you think you can take them out before they start shooting us?" Josh asked into the intercom. It was twice now they tried to take a member of the squad. The longer this went on, the stranger it all became.

"Yeah, I think I can handle the rest. I've been looking through the user manual. I think I found something that just might work," Cody replied and set his weapon for a wide angle. "Wide angle selected," an electronic voice said. Cody ignored it and aimed.

The silver wings detected the weapon and broke formation in opposite directions. Cody waited until the second they did and pulled the trigger. The cannon fired in a wide, thin spread beam that looked more like a laser light show.

As they changed directions, the blue light cut them in half, they started spewing red flames. They were still moving at full speed, and they all watched as the bottom, flaming shards of metal sailed through the air like comets, colliding with buildings. Buildings that still had lights.

Cody winced a little and looked away. He knew he might

have killed people, but there was no time to worry about what couldn't be changed.

"Not your fault," Josh said, and Cody didn't agree with that. It was time to get back to the situation at hand. "We are already down a member, well, half a member, I guess, but I suggest we get off this train before we attract any more attention," Josh said.

"That's a great idea. Someone should tell Blake," Dustin replied.

Dustin turned to look at Cody but was paying attention to something else. "The situation is getting worse. This fancy armor is intercepting reports that the harbor is filling up with mechanized ships. The navy is responding, but the battle isn't going well as we'd like," Cody said.

"This may as well be the damned end of the world if we don't do something. We need to find the source of this and end it quick," Dustin replied.

Cody didn't know what to do. There was no way to track the source, and no information was coming from the Syndicate. They were on their own.

"Machines run hot, and these things must have an impressive energy source to run like they do. Do a scan and locate the biggest source of power you can find ahead of us. We will go there. It shouldn't be too hard since the city's power grid is unstable," Cody suggested.

"Ha, why didn't I think of that? It was in my wheelhouse, I should have," Dustin said, playing it off like a joke, but it worried him a little that the thought never even occurred.

"Shouldn't we look for Wyatt? Who knows how many of those things are out there? He didn't do so well against them last time and--" Cody stopped him. "No. The mission is more important. The lives of millions are at stake, and we can't stop now," Josh looked away, not agreeing with this.

"It's not right. We'd come back for you," he said, trying to reason with him.

"No, you wouldn't come back for me because, as a member

of the team, you'd know that we all knew the job was dangerous and what it might mean in the end. Also, if you came back for me, I'd kill you for abandoning the mission. Wyatt is Delta. He can take care of himself," Cody said and walked past him as he put his weapon back at his side. "Blake, do a heat scan of the city if you can. I'm coming to you," Cody said as he walked.

Dustin and Josh looked back in the direction that Wyatt fell as it slid into the dark. "He'll be fine," Josh said and forced himself to turn back around in the direction they were going. "Yeah, just fine," Dustin added as they both made their way to the front.

"You wanted a scan? Well, I have good and bad news," Blake said, but Cody wasn't in the mood for games. "Just report what you found," Cody replied. "Good news: we are going in the right direction. Bad news: the strongest heat signature I can find is coming from the top of the Bank Tower," Blake said, and Cody looked up and saw the building in the distance.

"Contact the Syndicate. Tell them what we know and where we are going," Cody couldn't believe the source of this disaster was on top of such an obvious place, but at least they had an objective now.

## 27

"Are they coming yet?" she asked as she stood on the edge of the roof of the Bank Tower, staring down into the lights of the city and the rising smoke in various places. "Yes, they are on their way here. They know where we are, but are you sure this is a good idea?" he asked as he uncrossed his metal arms.

"Yes. I've always wanted to meet the Squad, face to face. I've heard such amazing stories," she said, turning around and hopping back from the edge. "Your Zeron science guys did some great work. They didn't even need much help from me," she said, still impressed at the whole thing.

The machine flinched a little. "Feelings are for humanity, and they only lead to self-destruction. You and I, we will make a better race, where true equality will become a reality and this human stain will be washed away once and for all," he said with a laugh, but it was a disturbing electronic sound that came out, not human laughter. It made her cringe while it lasted. So much for no feelings, she thought.

"Yeah, something like that, I suppose," she replied and turned back to the city below. Race and humanity never concerned her much. She was more interested in revenge against the Syndicate than anything or at least as much as she knew about them anyway.

"Can you tell me now, it's just the two of us," he asked as he walked next to her. "You know I don't like to talk about it," she replied.

"I know you're thinking about it. Come on, Dawn, I've never once heard the whole story, and what better time than now, waiting for them?" he asked, and she sighed. "I guess if you have to know," she replied. Then she decided to start at the beginning.

"I used to be average. No one would have looked at me twice walking down the street. I was fine with blending in. No one knew how much of a freak I really was," she said and swallowed. "The first thirteen years of my life were normal, I swear it. On my fourteenth birthday, something changed. One day I got mad, I don't even remember about what now, but in a fit of rage, I threw up my hands and my bed frame turned liquid. It melted, but without heat, you know? Of course, you know that much," she said.

"Parents freaking out, I was freaking out. You can only imagine how it was, but instead of thinking I was demonic or something, we decided to do our best to figure this out and did the thing average people do: we went to the hospital," she said with a laugh.

"They thought I was crazy, they thought we were all crazy, at least until I melted the doctor's chair in a fit of frustration. That got their attention. Then they did each test they could think of. You know this story. Everyone who's ever read a stupid comic book knows this story," she said. "Of course, I'm normal, if you go by those tests," she finished.

"That doctor must have talked to someone. Four days later, men in black raided my house. Before I could do anything, they hit me with something plastic. A dart, I suppose. The last thing I saw was my parents getting gunned down, my brother too. The gunfire still echoes in my nightmares, even now," she said, anger flashing in her eyes.

"When I woke up, I was in a pure white room. There were two scientists. Both women, one with brown hair, the other blonde. Both white-skinned demons, as far as I was concerned. With no metal in the room, I was helpless, scared, and all the rest of the emotions," she said. "I mean, I don't even know why the rest of this is important," she said but kept going anyway.

"Every day they injected me with something strange. It burned each time. I was stuck in that place for ten years. I'd find that out later. All those times I tried to escape, I'd almost get electrocuted to death, I think, by something I couldn't see," she said. "How did you get out?" he asked.

"Metal dust. The scientists started to get careless. Every time they brought something in for me to test, I'd make sure that I kept a little for myself. Over time, I even started to hear whispers of something called the Delta Squad when they thought I was sleeping. I even learned the name of the people keeping me: the Syndicate," she said.

"Anyway, you know the rest. I made my way out, killed the two women on my way out. When I discovered I was on an island, I ripped metal from their base and used it to get out. I flew as far as I could go before, I hit my limit and landed on your island, and here we are," she said. "Are you happy now?" she asked.

"Machines don't get happy, but if I were still human, I'd say yes," he replied.

She raised her hand, and from the roof rose liquid metal that solidified into a chair. She sat down.

"Waiting is boring," she said and watched as he paced back and forth, like a person would. He used to be one, she knew that, but it was still funny to watch anyway. "I hope they get here and aren't taken out by the machines first. That would be a shame, don't you think?" he asked as he paced.

"Yeah, but I have a feeling they'll be just fine," Dawn replied.

# 28

Wyatt pushed the machine corpse off him with ease and stood up, amazed that he was still able to move in this armor. He realized that he was in a bad part of town, but he didn't know where he was.

They could be heard in the dark, clanking around to various places. He didn't want to attract any attention, so he dashed off to the side and leaped to the roof of a house with ease to get a better vantage point of his surroundings.

He watched as people were being dragged from their houses and toward one of these shed things he saw before. One by one, people were thrown into the converters and in seconds stumbled out the other side with a strange silver metal growing through them as if it were a plant.

The people screamed for a short time before whatever this metal infection was took over. The screaming stopped. The knights had this process down to an art, but the children weren't acceptable for the transformation process for whatever reason.

Wyatt watched as the metal monsters tore them away from their families and, with ease, twisted their heads around as they screamed, like butchering a chicken, then tossed their bodies onto a growing pile.

Wyatt could hear the snap of their little necks from here over the wailing and screaming, and he couldn't take it anymore.

"There is no God, just me."

He drew his blade and leapt into the chaos, and everyone saw him. Everything stopped.

This was unforgivable by anyone's standards. Wyatt didn't even think about it when he sliced the transformation booth in half with one swing of his blade, and it didn't even explode, fell apart and hit the ground.

Wyatt was furious and needed to make this right somehow. No, that wasn't possible. There was no right to this, not anymore.

"Alright, you metal bastards. I don't know what you are, but I know what you are going to be in about five seconds," Wyatt said. Then he looked around. The people saw him but didn't know what to think and realized his mistake.

On one hand, the problem needed to be taken care of, on the other hand, these were all people they knew. Also, Wyatt's sudden appearance in full armor was something he wasn't supposed to be seen by the public eye, and here he was. He pushed the thought from his mind and prepared to kill everything with metal in it.

"If you're still human, run," Wyatt yelled out to the crowd in his alien voice.

For a minute, nobody was moving, still in shock. He looked down at his leg when a little girl was there, pounding on his leg fearlessly, trying to get his attention. He looked at her, breaking his concentration.

"You can't kill my daddy, you can't! I won't let you do it. I won't," she was pleading with him. He didn't know her name or who she was, or that she even existed before today. Her desperate eyes told him all he needed to know, and it was breaking his heart to do what had to be done next, but there was no choice.

"What are you people waiting for? Find shelter, hide," he

yelled again. This time the people turned and started to run into the unknown. For all Wyatt knew, there could have been machines waiting in the dark. At least he gave them a chance.

Not her, she was still latched onto Wyatt's leg in desperation. "You can't hurt them. Promise me, you can't hurt them," she pleaded with him.

He knelt to her as the machine horde was already advancing with heavy footsteps. His helmet slid back, revealing his face. "Listen. I know you might not understand what is going on, but you have to run now, please," he said.

Wyatt raised his blade to block the incoming metal hands. She screamed, being this close to the enemy, and there was no time left.

"Run," he ordered her as his helmet slid back on over his head. She turned and ran as he pushed the monster away. "Now you all pay," he said and concentrated on fighting. His sword grip tightened, and he swung his blade as hard as he could straight up between the legs of one of the infected, cutting through her lengthwise in one single stroke, sending blood up into the sky. He retracted back into a defensive stance and looked at his blood-covered blade and felt terrible, but the emotions could wait.

This whole situation was insane, and the only way to get through this was to let go of humanity. These weren't people anymore.

As he looked into their eyes, he could see their desperation and pain as the organic steel infested them. "I don't know who did this to you, but I'll put you out of your misery. I promise it'll be quick at least," he said to them. He had no idea if they understood or not.

## 29

The battle damaged train came to a stop far before the intended station. "I still think getting off here is a bad idea. Who knows what will be waiting for us," Blake said as he let go of the controls.

"Speaking of here, does anyone know where we are?" Dustin asked.

"Does it really matter? We know where the enemy is and—" Cody stopped and turned. "Do you hear that?" he asked. It was obvious now that the sounds of battle were closer here than anywhere else.

"God damn it, can't anything go right today?" Josh asked. The sounds of rapid gunfire were obvious now.

"The military is trying to take Downtown, and we walked right into their operation. The only reason they aren't over here yet is because they are either losing or winning," Dustin said, and Josh looked at him.

"Shut up already, just stop talking," Josh said and resisted the urge to punch him.

"Come on, let's go see what the damage is. Let's go back to the roof," Blake said, lifting his arm and firing a zip line into a nearby building and being pulled up. Cody was going to say something about it, but it was a good idea.

"Well, let's go," he said and followed Blake. The others did the same.

They got to the roof in seconds and didn't need to get any closer. "Well, looks like I was right," Dustin said, crossing his arms.

"Yeah, but who gave this order? It's a wasted mission," Cody asked and watched.

The sound of gunfire was endless. The knights were immune to rifle fire and kept moving forward. The infected humans were torn to shreds by the weapons. Their red blood had flecks of silver in it that reflected in the moonlight a little.

The squad watched as the knights returned fire with their thin green eye beams that cut through everything they touched. Soldiers were screaming, diving for cover to escape the sweeping death beam.

"It's a stalemate for now, but we can't depend on that to last," Cody said, looking at the situation.

"You call this a stalemate? How are we going to get around this?" Dustin asked, finally asking a relevant question, and no one had an answer.

As they watched the battle rage below, none dared wonder why the enemy wasn't using the rooftops to their advantage because as soon as they did, that was what was going to start happening.

"We could go up and over. The main threat is on the top of that tower, way, way up at the top of the thousand-foot tower," Dustin said. Blake realized that presented a problem too and continued.

"Cody, unless you can fly, we can assume the tower is filled to the brim with these things, and maybe even worse. Suggestions?" Blake pointed out. Cody didn't have a way forward, but it would come to him, but not before Dustin spoke up.

"I got a plan. We'll jump across from the building over there," Dustin said and pointed to the glass-covered building nearby, the top of which was on fire.

"You want us to climb that, and just jump across and hope we get lucky enough to not be seen or end up being spare parts on the pavement when we miss?" Josh said in disbelief, finally speaking up.

"That's as good a plan as any other. Let's go," Cody said, agreeing with Dustin much to the amazement of the others.

"Alright then, let's do it, I guess," Josh said but wasn't about to waste more time arguing about it now.

"I got nothing," Dustin said, looking for a way across.

"I do. Move on my mark," Cody said and pulled out his cannon, took aim at an armored transport on the ground. Then he pulled the trigger. The bright blue beam hit the vehicle, and it exploded with a flash so bright that all around it were blinded.

"God damn," Josh said, surprised he'd turn his weapon on the military like that.

"Now," Cody said at once, and the four of them ran at top speed, leaped off the roof, and landed in the middle of the street near the bright flames. Without missing a mark, they sped into the building in just the span of a few seconds.

The building didn't have a single intact pane of glass left. The place was a mess, and it was pitch black inside. The only light was from the fires of battle that made the shadows dance on the walls.

"No elevator. It looks like it's the stairs," Dustin said and continued, "I hate stairs," Dustin said, and Josh's eye twitched at the statement.

"Is it just me, or does it feel like we are being watched in here?" Blake asked as he looked around but saw nothing. The only sounds were the sounds of battle outside and wind whistling through the broken panes of glass.

"Well, after you. It was your idea. You get to climb the scary doom tower first. If the monster eats you, we will be sure to avenge your death in a timely fashion," Blake said to Dustin. He turned to glare at him, but Cody was on board with this idea.

"You heard the man. Your plan, you take point," Cody said, and Dustin grunted, turned around, and walked towards the stair entrance.

"Ten bucks says he gets eaten by the monster," Josh said with a smile in his voice.

"I'll take your money. There can't possibly be anything horrible up there lurking in the dark waiting for us. I'm sure it's safe. We'll be right behind you," Cody said sarcastically and laughed. None of this was making Dustin feel any better about his plan.

None of them wanted Dustin behind them after what he did earlier. It was always best to keep him in sight at all times.

## 30

The communication problem between Blackfire Island and the squad had not been fixed, but they could be seen on the map. "Why are they climbing that building, and where's Wyatt?" Heath asked, staring at their movements until it hit him. "They are going to try to jump it. What in the hell is wrong with them?" Heath asked and was furious with their so-called plan in an instant.

"Relax, I'm sure there was no other way. Look at the battle going on the street below them. It was the logical thing to do," Erin said. "Also, remember when we were out there in the battle, sometimes we just had to improvise? It usually turned out alright," she finished.

Heath turned and looked at her.

"Like the time you blasted into a death trap and we lost you for days and we barely found you alive? Other than that? Yeah, stupid plans work out all the time," Heath replied, and Erin pushed the blonde hair away from her eyes.

"Hey, no one's perfect, but they have the armor, the skills. I'm sure they'll be fine," Erin said, and Heath sighed then, knowing it was pointless to get worked up over it. There was nothing he could do, and she was right. They had to trust them.

"Guys, we have two infected specimens coming in. Two of our agents managed to recover two bodies, and we are teleporting them here soon. Erin, get to medical lab two," Emily said through the intercom.

"Yeah, I have plans for the holidays, so do try and figure out what these things are so we can kill them faster," Heath said and kept his eyes on the big screen.

"Yeah, I'll do that," she said but already had a good idea of what she was going to find in the investigation. Heath watched as the squad made their way up the building in record time.

"Good luck," he said to no one, hoping for the best because it was all he could do from here.

He couldn't believe this had turned into such a mess, and worse, he couldn't believe they missed all of this. How did this get past their surveillance? One would think an army of machines would be something hard to miss. Heath began to wonder if someone on his side wasn't responsible for this, and maybe the communication issues too.

The paranoia was beginning to creep up on him.

## 31

The four of them stood on the top of the building. The night air was filled with the smoke and sounds of battle, firelight coming from below. "So, we just jump across, seems easy enough," Dustin said and then looked over to the Bank Tower and judged the distance. It was farther than any other they had come across.

"I don't think this is going to work, but an order is an order all the same, so it looks like it's time, hell. I'll even go first," Dustin walked backward to what he hoped was a good enough distance, then he took off running towards the edge with no warning or hesitation while Cody was talking to the rest of the team.

"See, jumping was just a joke. I'm sure we can just use the zip lines to-" Cody turned around in time to watch Dustin leap off the building at full power.

"That boy ain't right," Josh said as he watched Dustin fly off the edge.

"So, do we save him or see if he makes it?" Blake asked as they watched him sail towards the building.

"He'll have to catch up. If he turns into street pizza, we'll send a cleanup crew later to peel him off," Cody said.

They watched Dustin slam into a much lower floor window and through it. "Alright guys, I made it. All you need to do is jump at the last second and you'll make it, no problem," Dustin said into his communicator as he watched the lines fire from the opposite roof and into a much higher floor, and then one by one he watched them all get pulled across on their zip lines.

"Oh right, we can do that." He said and couldn't believe he jumped off a skyscraper. "Enjoy the climb up, bitch," Josh said with a laugh. Dustin rolled his eyes. He was about to have an epic comeback when he heard a metallic growl come from behind him and turned around.

In the dark, there were two yellow glowing eyes watching him.

"Oh, hello there, who are you supposed to be, or what?" Dustin asked it and was careful not to make any sudden movements. The thing melted out of the darkness and into the light. It was a pure machine with silver skin, with fangs of steel and claws to match. It was a large metal cat.

It screamed at him with an unearthly roar. The intruder needed to die. The message was clear to Dustin. "Guys, I have a little problem," Dustin said.

"You are a problem, deal with it and meet us up here," Josh replied. "Thanks for that," Dustin replied.

The two stared one another down when the metal cat lunged at him, but Dustin sidestepped, spun with the thing. He watched it sail out the window. "Goodbye, kitty," he said and started to walk into the dark, but behind him he heard a noise, a clawing noise, and stopped in his tracks.

"Can't anything go right for a change?" Dustin said as he turned around to see the metal cat was climbing through the window and even if it was a machine, it didn't look happy.

"Nice kitty, maybe we can make a deal?" he asked as he prepared for a fight.

## 32

Wyatt had his hands full. He intended to kill all of the infected people and the machines that caused this all at the same time. His rage turned to worry when from every direction these infected people began to walk from behind the houses.

Before he knew it, he was surrounded by the horde.

"Damn it," Wyatt said and tightened his grip. He decided to attack first and couldn't afford to hold anything back.

He lunged towards the first infected person and shoved his blade deep into his chest. Blood and blue ooze sprayed from the wound, but Wyatt had no time to hesitate. He pulled out the blade and dashed to his left and sliced through the neck of another and it fell to her knees. Wyatt was thankful they had the same weaknesses as normal people. As he moved to his next target, one lunged at him and took him by surprise.

He had no idea what they were capable of. It grabbed him by the throat and slammed him to the ground. Even with his armor, the wind got knocked out of him on impact.

He retaliated by swinging the blade with all his power and cutting off the arm at the elbow and rolling away. That metal-infected arm refused to let go of his neck on its own. "Get off of me," he said and pulled it off, throwing it to the ground. The thing started to pull itself in his direction with its fingers. It creeped him out.

These things mindlessly walked towards him. They didn't run and that made it worse, but he didn't know why.

Wyatt walked back then bumped into something. He tensed and looked behind him, expecting a metal demon, but it was a wall. There was a building behind him. "That's why you're not running. I was stupid enough to get myself trapped," he said at about the same time their eyes began to glow blue.

It didn't take him long to figure out what was going to happen next, and he took a quick step forward. "Wait for it," he said.

At the same time the machines fired their blue eye beams, Wyatt leapt as high as he could with a slight angle back. He landed on the roof of the house as the beams tore into it. The horde seemed endless from the ground, but in reality, there were fifteen of them.

They looked up to where he went a second later and those cutting, thin beams followed him. Wyatt jumped into the air again, straight up. This time he took a chance and blocked four of the beams with his blade and angled it back at the enemies as he flew through the air.

The beams reflected at a wide angle and struck the infected humans down where they stood. With no self-preservation instincts left, he watched as the beams sliced through the horde.

Wyatt's blade was red hot for a few seconds as he landed. Behind him, his enemies fell to the ground, sliced into pieces at the slightest vibration. He didn't bother turning around to look at any of them because he was sure if he missed any they would have attacked by now.

"Man, I am way better than anyone thinks I am," he said, kind of wishing he had an audience for that because it would likely never happen again. He won, but he didn't feel good about it. Those used to be people hours ago, people with lives and all that other stuff. Now they were abominations on the ground, mixed with the monsters that made them this way, all in pieces.

Wyatt did a quick search with his armor and it told him where the others were. He put his blade away and knew he was going to be late for the party at Bank Tower.

He took off running in their direction but had no idea what he might be running into. He knew it was going to take him a while because after what he had seen, there was no way he was going to allow a single infected person to escape again.

## 33

Dustin fired and the bullets tore through the metal skin with ease, but unlike anything else he had met before, the damage was repaired as it was inflicted. Dustin was more than a little surprised. The bullets were enough to knock it down, but it got up again. It reminded Dustin of a song. He could almost hear it, but not quite.

"What the hell are you?" he screamed as the cat lunged at him. Dustin grabbed the forearms of the beast. They both went through the wall into the other room, collapsing on the floor. The claws of the metal cat grazed Dustin's helmet as he fell.

"Bad kitty, very bad," he said and put his legs under it and kicked the thing so hard it slammed into the ceiling as Dustin rolled away, getting back on his feet.

"Fine, you don't seem to want to die the easy way, I'll just beat you to death," Dustin said and somehow figured that if his gun wouldn't work, his fists would do the job.

He charged the cat and put his right fist into its face. The force of the attack sent the thing into the air and back through the wall to the adjacent room. Dustin's armor was thick, but he still thought he felt his bones crack under the impact. The sharp pain he felt disappeared as he noticed it.

The metal cat wasted no time in jumping right back through the hole. Without thinking about it, he raised his left arm to block the thing, but the claws on its right arm sliced right through his armor and drew blood.

He was surprised and the pain was immediate. He threw his arm to the side and the cat was almost thrown back out the window but hit the wall instead. Dustin rushed forward, grabbed the beast's neck, picked it up and slammed it into the ground. The floor was beginning to crack under the strain of battle.

"The day I get eaten by a machine is the day I quit the team," Dustin said, letting his rage take control. The cat tried to fight but Dustin was picking it up by its neck and slamming it into the floor. Over and over, harder each time. "Just die," he said as he crushed it into the floor.

It roared at him. As it did this, Dustin lifted his right hand and stuck it into the mouth of the cat and unleashed his wrist flame thrower. Flames erupted from every joint of the thing and within seconds it fell limp to the floor. He tore his hand out and looked at the wrecked metallic cat.

"There it took some doing but I did it, you're history," Dustin said as he stood up and turned to begin his long trek up the building when he heard the distinctive sound of grinding metal. "No way." He stopped in his tracks, turned around, and the cat was twitching.

"What does it take to kill you?"

He held up his flamethrower and pointed it at the cat as it returned to life, but at the sight of the weapon, it retreated to the corner, dragging melted pieces that hung from it.

Dustin did not pull the trigger as he was confused at what he saw. "This is impossible. How can a computer be afraid?" Dustin knew what fear looked like in the eyes of the living but had never seen it before in the eyes of a robot.

"What kind of program is this?" he asked himself, lowered his weapon as he approached the thing. He knelt down in front of it, he expected it to attack, but it didn't. Dustin reached out and put his hand on the top of the metal cat's head, and it recoiled in fear, expecting to die. Dustin thought now that this was some kind of a trick. It would attack at any second, drawing him in close. He was tense, but curious too. There was a sound coming from behind him.

He turned to look There was something metal that was trapped under a piece of the wall. He walked over and kicked the junk off, and the metal flew towards the cat to disappear in its body somewhere.

For a machine, expecting anything was something of a miracle. "I won't hurt you anymore, but there is so much I don't understand and doesn't even make sense. What are you?" he asked, knowing the threat was over but not sure how or why.

"You stay here. I'll be back for you," he said and turned and began to walk away. He took two steps when he heard the sound of heavy footsteps following him and he stopped, looked over his shoulder to see the metal tiger following him.

"Fine, if you have to come with me, but you'll need to take care of yourself," he said to it, and the thing didn't seem to mind.

"I'll call you Sparky," Dustin said, and the cat didn't seem to mind the name either. The two of them began to make their way up to the others.

## 34

The three squad members made it to the roof of the tower. "Well, you know what they say, leaders go first," Blake said. "Yeah, they do," he replied and stepped through the door. It could have been trapped, but Cody had a feeling it wouldn't be. Whoever was behind this was a fan of being theatrical.

There was no one up here besides two figures in the distance. They were sitting in metal thrones. "Great," Josh said as he stepped out on the roof.

The team walked right up to them to see what this was all about.

"Well, you made it, took you all night to get here, but you did," he said and stood up.

"Aren't you missing two?" she asked after he stood up. "The stories always said they had five members, not three. Is this some kind of battle tactic or what?" She didn't get up to meet them but was wary of this new development.

"The other two are out sick, but that's okay. We only need three to get the job done. I'm afraid you have us at a disadvantage. You seem to know us, but we don't know who you are, you could at least introduce yourselves before we kill you," Cody said and crossed his arms. He didn't like to kill people he didn't know, even on a mission.

"I guess introductions wouldn't hurt. My name is Josh, and the lovely lady with the silver skin here is Dawn, but I suppose people like you need fancier names. You can call me Dead Steel and she's the Silver Queen. Now since that is out of the way, maybe we can get down to the business of killing you," Dead Steel said, and even if his body was like the machines from earlier, he was acting like a person would. It was strange to combine the two realities.

"The woman's alive, the metal is like a second skin. I can detect life underneath. The other one is all metal," Blake said through the intercom. "Good to know," Cody replied.

"Can we just kill them now?" Blake asked. "Sure, why not?" Josh replied and prepared his weapons to fight.

Dead Steel raised his right hand and stopped them. "Wait, hold on. Killing us won't stop them. You see, there are power cores. Five of them hidden across the city, each one energizes a piece of the army. Take these out, and you'll win. But there is a catch. At this time tomorrow or so, the Protobots will be separated from the cores and be fully charged, therefore unstoppable," the metal man said and laughed as he wrapped his black coat around him. "Goddamned timed fetch quest," Josh said under his breath.

"Wait, protobots? That is the stupidest name I have ever heard. You couldn't have come up with anything better? Cybermen, Terminators, Borg, Robot Masters?" Blake asked and shook his head in disappointment.

"Nope. Protobots. It's the best name of all time, and they are going to kill all of you, and then everyone will be converted to perfection," Dead Steel proudly proclaimed.

She looked over and shook her head in embarrassment, he wasn't paying attention. Then stood beside him.

"It is because of your people this is happening. The Syndicate will pay for this, and it will start with your deaths," Dawn said.

"Lady, none of us know who you are," Cody replied. "Is revenge really the reason for all of this?" Josh asked.

Dawn felt that, how infuriating. They didn't even know who she was. They were going to learn today. She fought back the urge to impale all of them right here, still fearing some kind of trap if she did. They walked through that door with too much confidence not to be prepared.

"They could be lying, I mean protobots? Are you serious?" Josh said the obvious.

"Yes, but if they aren't a battle here might be pointless. There is no way to do a citywide scan either to find out without contact with the Island," Blake said and wanted nothing more than to shoot Dead Steel in the face.

"Yeah, two members down and five targets," Cody didn't know what to do but wasting time in combat was a good distraction and would be what the two of them wanted, but why would they bother telling them about these cores in the first place? It made no sense.

"Time is ticking, Squad, what's it going to be?" Dead Steel asked.

"I say we kill them now, nothing's stopping us," Blake said. "It shouldn't take long," Josh replied. Dawn didn't think this is how it was going to go. She thought for sure that this plan would work.

"You guys don't get it. If something happens to either of us, the protobots will be unleashed now. You'll never catch them. They'll spread this metal plague. Is that a chance you want to take?" she said in a hurry.

"That really sounds like something you just made up right now. I think you're lying," Josh replied. Cody rolled his eyes.

"Damn it, you might be right, but is that a chance we need to take?" Cody asked. Blake still wanted to get it over with.

"We can catch these robots, let's do this already," Blake said. Dawn did her best to not act scared. It was then Cody got an idea.

"Dustin, are you still alive?" he asked into the intercom. "Yeah, I'm almost there. What is it?" he replied, sounding annoyed.

"Alright, listen. New information has come in, but there is no way to know if it's true or not. Do you have a scanner powerful enough for the whole city? We need to know if there are five power sources bigger than the rest," Cody said.

Dustin stopped in his tracks as he heard this. "I have no idea, standby, I'll check," he replied.

Dustin turned on his scanner to full power and walked to the nearest window, punched it out with one swing of his right hand. "Alright, do your thing," he said to no one. He looked around for a second from where he was, soon enough, there were five beacons of power lighting up across the city. Not one of them was close.

"Damn it, Commander. Why do you always have to complicate things? All we had to do was kill the bad guy. Yes, there are five sources of power, but they are far from here in every direction. If I didn't know better, it was designed to split us up, and I am transmitting the locations to you now," Dustin was pissed, and he looked at Sparky.

"Well, welcome to the Squad, I guess," the cat tilted its head, confused.

Cody took a breath once he saw what Dustin did and believed them. "Fine, don't leave town because if you do, we'll hunt you down to the ends of the earth for as long as it takes," Cody said. Josh almost lost his temper.

"Goddamned fetch quests," he said, crossing his arms.

"You have our word. We'll have our battle if you can save the world," she said. It was the tone of her voice and the way she said it that made Cody believe her. "Then we have a deal," Cody replied, and there was one more thing to do.

"Okay, here's the plan. We each take a target and split up in the infected city to go find enemies that may or may not exist, kill them and meet back here," Cody said and continued in his intercom.

"Guys, it's going to be a long day. We either succeed and meet back here this time tomorrow, or nothing will matter anymore. Wyatt, I don't know where you are. If you can hear me, find a target and mark it. Good luck out there," he said and finished.

Cody hated it when he didn't know the status of his team. He tried to locate him from here, but there was no signal to locate. Cody put that aside for now and focused on the mission at hand.

"Commander, are you sure we should try to take these on our own? They are obviously traps, it can't be this easy. We should kill them now while we're here," Blake said one more time. Cody turned to look at him.

"Funny, I thought you were a member of the squad. You can work on your own as well as on a team. We need to do this, and we need to stop wasting time, that's final," Cody replied, his mind made up.

"Sorry for thinking, I'll get right on it," Blake said. Cody didn't like the tone but didn't press the issue. He turned to face the two of them. "Soon," he said as he cloaked himself and ran towards the edge of the roof. He leapt off the side of the thousand-foot tower and pointed his wrist towards a building, fired his zip line.

"Thinking is overrated anyway," Cody said as he watched him jump.

Josh said nothing. He was annoyed with his brother's choice. He turned and walked off in the opposite direction Blake did.

"What? Are you mad too? Come on, man, it's not like we have a choice," Cody said. Josh wasn't having it. He walked to the edge of the roof and jumped off, disappearing in the dark.

Cody knew splitting up was the right thing to do. He had to make the hard choices and take responsibility. If this was the end of the world, it was the right choice.

He took one last glance at the metal pair and pointed at them.

"We'll see you again. Like I said, don't leave town," he said and lowered his arm. With that, he walked straight back and leapt off the edge of the building as well, taking the third direction.

Dawn and Dead Steel waited for a few seconds in silence. "Oh my god, I can't believe they bought that," she said, letting out a breath. "Right, I can't believe it worked. I had no idea you could come up with a plan so quick," Dead Steel replied.

"I guess you never know what you can come up with until you stare death in the face," she replied, still in disbelief that trick worked. "The white one was right, protobots is a dumb name," she said, and Dead Steel looked at her. "I was trying to be original, sorry, you can name the next ones," he replied, and she smiled.

## 35

Wyatt stopped on the roof of a house and watched his screen. One by one the targets began to light up, each one matched with the color of each armor. Wyatt noticed his and saw it was the one farthest away.

"Well, thanks guys," he said and looked around for enemies, but he didn't see anything close by. "Fine, I guess I'll go that way, jerks. You could have left me an easy one because—" Wyatt was cut off.

"If you keep whining, I will find and hurt you. Turn off your intercom when you monologue," Josh said in an uncomfortably angry voice.

"Well, okay, I didn't know it was still on. Sorry," Wyatt replied and turned off the intercom.

"Better get started," he said. Wyatt looked to the left and wasn't sure what to do. On one hand he wanted to get the mission over with. On the other, he'd seen the nightmare that was unfolding up close.

He thought about it and decided to damn the time limits and stepped off the roof. He decided to take the streets as long as he could, kill any infected he found, and take as many of the machine invaders as he could on the way there.

Dustin was still in the building. The metal cat was insistent on continuing up the stairs, but Dustin couldn't go that way.

"Yeah, Sparky, I understand what you're saying. Kill the bad guy and go home, but the commander sometimes, well, he just doesn't make any sense. Let's get going," he said to his new friend and walked towards the exit from the stairwell.

It led him into a hallway, and he took the first door to his left. The room was someone's office this time, pictures on the desk, papers, and other things he didn't care about. Dustin slid the desk over to the left side of the room with ease. The metal cat entered the room beside him. "Let's go," he said and kicked the window out. As soon as it broke, the wind rushed in.

He looked at the cat and shook his head. "This is where you get off, I guess," Dustin said and jumped out the window towards the building. He fired his zip line to catch the wall. It hit, and he swung to the side, and he heard a click.

He turned to look, and he saw the cat leap off the edge, and Dustin was shocked, but he was even more shocked when the metal cat's paws exploded with fire and Sparky began to fly. "Well, you're full of surprises," Dustin said and began to retract the line. Sparky blasted past him to land on the roof. "Wait for me," Dustin said, also wishing he could fly. It would have made life much easier.

He made a mental note to add that feature to the next version of the armor.

Blake hated all of this. Running from the enemy in the direction of an obvious death trap was so stupid. He landed on a roof, and the distant pounding of metal footsteps came from below. Blake stood on the edge of that building and saw people in various stages of transformation marching down the street.

Blake turned his head, and from the other direction, he saw soldiers sweeping streets, and for whatever reason seemed oblivious to the thundering footsteps coming in their direction. It must have been the sounds of battle that were growing all over the city in the night that covered them up.

He had his orders, but this was going to be a massacre. Blake could see them, but what caught his attention were the two knights they had in their company. If he could take them out, this battle might turn out differently. He pulled out his sniper rifle and took aim.

Blake pulled the trigger, and he watched as the bullet bounced off the knight. "Son of a bitch," he said, disappointed in how that turned out. The machines didn't even register it as an attack. It was clear he needed to try something else.

He flipped a switch on the side of his gun and took aim again. "Alright, robot or whatever you're supposed to be, it's time to be scrap metal," Blake said and realized that he wasn't good with words and should stick with shooting.

He fired again, and the bullet hit the head of the knight and stuck to it. Blake changed his aim and fired again at the second. The bullet did the same thing, and the two of them stopped at the same time, as if they couldn't figure out what was wrong.

"Goodbye," Blake said and pushed a button on the side of his rifle. The bullets exploded with such force it took the heads of the machines off, sending dark blue blood and metal shards in all directions.

The metal things fell to their knees and dropped dead. Blake thought he helped the situation, but in his focus, he failed to scan for other life. The buildings on the side came to life, the soldiers already had an ambush planned, and Blake knew he wiped out the element of surprise and backed out of sight. He was sure no one saw him, reasonably sure anyway.

The gunfire erupted below him.

Blake tuned into their radio transmissions and listened to whatever came up that might have been important. He hoped no one saw what he did but he needed to be sure.

"Sarge, you think this is a good idea? Sure, we were paid, but these things don't even seem to care we are killing them, and what in the hell killed the two big ones anyway?" a man asked over the radio.

"This is the kind of situation those Delta guys show up on, you know? You suppose they are out here doing this too?" another guy with a deeper voice asked, then right away trying to talk over the sound of close gunfire.

"Will all of you shut up, please? The Delta Squad is a stupid a military legend, a story somebody made up over a hundred years ago, and it won't die. There is nobody out there better than us. We were paid to kill these things, so let's get it done," a man interjected and appeared to be the leader.

"Just make sure the Harrier is ready to go if we need it," he said and finished. The sound of gunfire made him hard to understand.

"Yeah, Strom, don't worry about it. Nobody even knows she's up there, it's cloaked," the first man said.

Blake looked up, and it was then he saw it through the flickering fire, smoke, and the light of the pale moon—the outline of a nearly invisible jet a few buildings away.

"Bingo, but how in the hell did they get something like that?" he asked himself, but didn't care so much. He knew what he wanted now and planned on getting it. His mission was about to get a lot easier.

The sniper was silent as he moved towards the building. He took a few steps back and took off running towards the edge and jumped. He made it about halfway when he fired the zip line and pulled himself to the other side.

Not missing a step, he pulled himself on the roof and started running towards the direction of the jet and repeated what he did.

Blake wanted to test how good his armor really was, so he walked between the center two as the one on the left pulled his rifle and aimed.

Blake looked at what they were aiming at, and it was no machine. These so-called soldiers were aiming at people who were running away down a side street. The other man joined him. "You said it."

Blake couldn't believe what he was hearing and grabbed both of their rifle barrels, one in each hand, and pointed their weapons to the sky with ease.

As the men's faces turned to looks of confusion, then horror.

"Well, you're both better off dead, right?" he asked and threw them off the edge of the building with ease into the street below. They managed to scream, but the constant gunfire made them impossible for anyone to hear.

Blake turned his attention to the other four and decided that they were all the same way. The remaining guards didn't even notice two of their own were thrown off in this chaos. They were all facing different directions.

He had a new plan. "Hey, guys. Aren't you missing somebody?" he asked them, and they turned around to see nobody, but two of their members had disappeared. "What? Who said that? Who's out there?" one of them said, looking around in all directions in a panic. The others were nervous at the sudden invasion.

One who appeared to be the leader took three steps forward to get a better look. He was stopped in his tracks when Blake's blade was thrust into the left side of his neck. Blood erupted from the wound, and the man fell dead. Blake at once jumped to the wing of the plane to avoid detection.

The last three began to open fire in the direction the man who died, hoping to hit something.

"Too easy," Blake said with a smile as he leapt down from the wing. His fist slammed into the top of the head of the one in the back. His metal fist tore through the skull before the body hit the floor and the blood rushed down the back of the man's black uniform. He grabbed the rifle before it hit the ground and shot the other two in the back of their heads.

"I hate mercenaries," he said and crushed the weapon in his hand, tossed it to the side, wiped the blood off his blade, and put it back where it belonged. It was an easy thing to climb into the jet after this and climb into the cockpit of the thing. His armor made for a tight fit, but he managed.

Blake wondered how the mercs got into the city. It was not with this. Then he wondered why he was caring so much. There were more important things to do.

"Just like riding a bike, you never really forget," he said and started the process. A few seconds later, the jet took off. Both were cloaked. Nobody saw them leave. He flew towards the target. It wouldn't take him long at all to get there in this thing.

From the air, he could see the city, and it was a terrible sight. There were fires breaking out in all directions. Large chunks of the city were black as the power had been knocked out. Some of the tallest buildings saw damage as well. None of this was looking like it was going to have a positive outcome.

Blake wanted to run up and down the streets to blast everything, but he had a mission. He thought it was strange he wasn't seeing more helicopters, but his question was answered when a group of those flying wings shot out of the darkness and shredded a helicopter that was in full retreat in the distance.

He was sure no one survived the explosion. He tried not to look anymore, hoped that they wouldn't see him, if only for a few minutes. It's all he would need to get where he was going in this thing.

Blake flew through the sky. The modified jet was able to avoid detection. He wasn't exactly sure how. In the distance, on the hill, were the letters that spelled Hollywood. Blake wasn't sure why one of the power sources would be here. He couldn't see anything obvious, but his armor was telling him that it was behind the letters.

Blake flew over the sign, and instantly a pair of bright blue beams sliced into his right wing. He pulled on the controls to spin the plane towards the direction of the attacker. "What the hell," Blake said as the sudden attack made him panic.

He scanned the ground and saw his attacker. "Missiles," Blake said as he looked for the switch, but to his disappointment, there was no switch for them. Just the guns remained on this thing. "Figures as much. They spent all their money on stealth," Blake said and took aim as he narrowly avoided another blue blast from the dark.

The guns on the Harrier unleashed their fury in the direction of the attacker as twin beams shredded his other wing and set it on fire at the same time. Blake didn't want to destroy the landmark. He veered his plane in the opposite direction as it fell. There was no time to eject, and the jet crashed into the hillside.

Blake tore open the rest of the hatch and stumbled out of the plane, landing in the dirt face first. His armor was on fire, and his cloak had been knocked offline.

He was alive but in pain as he pulled himself away from the flames. It became apparent that the sounds of footsteps were coming in his direction, the heavy metal kind. Blake tried to get up, but that wasn't working.

His armor was busy rebooting. All he could do was hear the coming footsteps and try not to think about all the broken bones mending in his body. "Come on, Blake, you've got to move faster," he said and tried to pull himself up and again collapsed to the ground.

"Why can't it be easy once?" he asked and realized he was helpless. The armor that saved his life was now the thing that was about to get him killed.

## 36

"Diamond Bar, I've never heard of it," Wyatt said as he stopped to look at where his target was for the first time and couldn't believe it. He was near downtown, and according to his armor, this new target was no less than twenty-seven long, machine-filled miles away.

"I hate you guys sometimes. I really do," Wyatt said and had no intention of running the entire distance. He looked around and discovered that all the modes of transportation around him were unreliable or so damaged that they looked like they were about ready to fall to pieces.

Violence took place here, but Wyatt didn't think it was battle damage, instead, the remains of a riot of people trying to get away.

There was no one here anymore, but no signs of the enemy or dead people. Everything looked as hopeless as he was starting to feel.

As he turned his head to the left, he spotted what looked like a wheel sticking out from under a crumbling wall. He moved to the scene and pulled the wall off, tossing it to the side with ease.

Underneath, there was a rather large motorcycle, covered in white dust, but it was intact.

Wyatt picked it up and saw that it was black and gold in color. It matched his armor well, and he liked it. "If you run, you'll do," he said in a half prayer that it would work out the way he wanted it to.

Wyatt didn't have keys, but his armor interfaced with the computer on the bike as soon as he touched it.

It only took a few seconds to get the thing started with a roar that echoed between the abandoned houses. Wyatt cringed at the noise. "Stealthy as hell," he said at the same time. Time was no longer on his side, and there were no other options.

Wyatt had no idea how to get where he was going. If it weren't for his armor, he'd have to do it the hard way, and he hated reading maps.

He started rolling down the road as his armor plotted the best path for him to follow. A yellow path painted on the road in front of him. It reminded him of a high-tech version of *The Wizard of Oz* and following the virtual yellow road. "Time to go hunt a witch," he said.

Too many things were running through his head as he increased his speed. Top on the list of those was wondering if he did the right thing with the infected people earlier. It was bugging him that he might be a mass murderer. It never occurred there might be a cure someday, if it was even possible.

He turned a corner and it was then an unsettling thought came to mind. It was December 19th, 2012.

The world was supposed to end in two days. Wyatt never put much stock in the theories of crazy people, but now it felt like the real deal. Wyatt steeled himself against the idea of a cybernetic apocalypse and increased his speed. The world wasn't going to end on his watch if he could help it, after all, his stuff was on the world.

As he moved down the path being laid out for him, he would glance to the left and the right to catch glimpses of battles as he sped past, things he wished he could stop but the priority had changed in the last few minutes.

Chaos was consuming the night and the city. It was becoming clear that it was going to be impossible to control any road in this city for long at the rate the enemy was advancing.

Wyatt couldn't stop for anything, not even the helicopter that showed up on the inside of his visor.

"Seriously, don't come this way," Wyatt said, as one might say when a circus clown approaches them as they wander aimlessly in a crowd. Wyatt was well aware that he looked mechanical in his armor, and to any military forces, that was more than enough to get shot at. Wyatt was moving at a high rate of speed and was visible to everyone.

The helicopter was getting closer, and he knew that he must have been spotted by now.

"I don't have time for you today, guys," he said. He knew they would do some recon work first. They needed to get a good look at him before they opened fire. "Oh, that'll do, flyboys, just don't get out of range," Wyatt said as they flew over him. The chopper turned around, and his armor tracked it. Then it told him that their guns were locked.

It moved into an attack vector before it began to fly in his direction to do a strafe and blast him into pieces. Wyatt waited until he could hear the gunfire. Then it was time to put this armor to the test. He got to his feet and jumped straight at the helicopter.

The pilots could only watch in amazement, or maybe horror, as the enemy landed on the front of the craft. At the same time, he drew his blade. To them, the thing that happened next was too fast for them to see.

He used the sword to cut through the spinning rotors that connected those spinning blades. Those blades went straight off into the black sky and the rest began to fall.

Wyatt jumped off the falling craft and landed back on the bike as it began to fall over and continued on his way. All he heard was the crash behind him but didn't bother to see if anyone was injured or not.

## 37

Josh hated big cities. His target was showing up on his internal map, and according to this, it was leading him in the wrong direction. It was in an infested part of the city where the attacks first started. It could have been somewhere quiet, but no, things never worked out that way.

His target was nearby, but it was on the street level. Josh stood on a rooftop and, above all else, he knew he needed a plan. Usually, all that was needed was to find someone to shoot at and the job was done.

The first thing he needed to do was get a good look at the target. All his internal scan was showing him was a big red mark on a digital map, and that was useless. Josh jumped off the roof and fired his zip line to attach himself to the next building in front of him and pulled himself up.

Below him on the street was a metal fortress. He saw machines in various states of transformation working on setting up and welding walls. The place was swarming with them. "Yeah, why not?" Josh asked himself and looked for a good way to attack without being surrounded, but the more he looked, the more he saw that this was impossible. He decided that the best approach was the direct one to take and leapt off the building.

He landed in the street with a green flash right behind a knight and pointed his wrists at the back of the machine before it could turn around and shot it. The thing fell to the ground with thick blue fluid spraying from the wounds. He crushed its head under his heavy metal foot to make sure it wouldn't get back up.

"It looked smaller from up there," Josh said as they turned to watch him from the safety of their walls. He took a deep breath and marched forward to the front gates of the place. About halfway to the black metal gates, he realized that no one was attacking him.

This was worse than a fight because now he knew something bad was about to happen, but what, he didn't know.

Once he was closer to the metal gates, to his surprise, the things started to scrape against the cement, opening up. "Well, thanks for the invitation, I guess," he said with his weapons at the ready and walked through the gates.

"Hello, brother," a deep red knight walked forward and spoke with a human voice. Josh didn't know they could talk and wasn't about to trust any of them.

"Hi, you have something I need," Josh replied to the machine in red, deciding to try and be civil for now. "Yeah, I know we do. I don't think you understand the situation. We need to talk," it replied and started walking.

Josh followed him but was aware that he was being watched by eyes he could feel were unfriendly and knew that there was nothing stopping them from all attacking at once. He wondered what it could possibly have to say.

"We call you a monster because your kind kills us. Look around. Don't you see that those fools created something and had no idea what they made? We are evolving. Sure, we are made from the inferior flesh of humans, but look at what we become. Killing us is the same as genocide, friend. Are you really a monster under that armor?" the red knight asked.

"No, I am not a monster, but I do have a mission. I don't want to kill you, really. I need what I came for," Josh replied, but he lied. He really did want to kill all of them on principle of being what they were.

"No, you don't understand. We know you came for our power source. Why else would you have found your way here after all? Without it, we will not lose this section of the city, but we will die as well. Without time to grow, we will all perish here."

Josh couldn't see them as evil now, but more like an infection that learned how to talk. But they were talking and reasonable, too. While he didn't expect that, he still wanted to wipe them out.

"Isn't there any way you can live without it?" he asked and hoped for the right answer.

"No, there isn't. If you take it now, we'll all be, as you people call it, dead. We are all connected to it here." It was not what he wanted to hear.

"Come, follow me. Let me show you what the source of our power is. Maybe that will change your mind and maybe even the entire thought process you have about us and who the real monsters really are," he said as they kept walking to the center of the twisted steel fortress.

Josh became a little bit nervous as they moved deeper into the enemy camp and farther away from anything resembling safety, not quite sure if the place he was being led to was somewhere he wanted to be.

# 38

Dustin was not happy, but that was normal. He picked a target without looking. It was like a mad dash for objectives at the time. He regretted his choice now that he had the time to see where it was. It was near the water, and he hated the water. His code name was Flame Genesis. He would have been happier in a wildfire, but if you play stupid games, you win stupid prizes, he supposed.

The battle below him still raged, and the first order of business was to get out of here without anyone paying attention to the giant orange thing. He took a running leap out of the broken window and fired.

One rooftop at a time, he managed to get away from the chaos, and as far as he knew, no one had seen a thing or the flying metal cat that followed him through the air.

He landed on another roof and looked over the edge. No one was there, no one was around either, and he was thankful for that. From here, the buildings became progressively shorter. He needed transportation, so he dropped off the side and landed on the street, cracking the sidewalk in the process.

"Well, Sparky, it looks like we're going to Santa Monica, I guess. Perfect place to go before Christmas," he said to the metal cat and looked at his map again, wondering how he was going to get there.

Dustin turned on his message log. He needed to record a message. "Guys, I'm making this as a recording in case I don't make it. If I get turned into one of those things, please be sure to kill me and burn all of my computers, thanks."

He shut off his recorder and looked to the metallic cat. "Well, we better get going. Do you think you can stay out of trouble?" he asked with a laugh. The cat didn't seem to understand a single word as it gazed off into the distance.

Wasting no time, Dustin started to walk down the street, Sparky at his side. There were plenty of cars around, but they were all tiny, and Dustin was sure that he could pick them up and throw them with one hand. It didn't make him feel any better.

"It looks like we are going to have to walk the whole way there because California doesn't like anything bigger than a Geo on their roads. Crazy," Dustin said to Sparky and was disappointed in the selections they were being presented with. It appeared people from California didn't like to drive anything much bigger than they were.

They turned a corner, and there was a silver truck, and it was in good condition. "Is it better to be smart or lucky?" Dustin asked with a smile and walked towards it, looking around for any signs of an ambush, but there didn't seem to be any machines. He didn't expect that to last much longer.

"It's not exactly stealthy, but it will have to do. I suppose it is going to take forever to get there, isn't it?" The cat blinked at him as he asked it. It had no idea what was going on.

"Right then, get into the back, and I'll drive. You can't drive and you're a cat," Dustin said and wished he could fly right about now. He walked up and opened the door to the driver's side. The door was locked, but he snapped it open with little effort. Tore the driver's seat out so he could fit and got in.

He found that the keys were not in it, but he wasn't too

worried about this. He thought about tearing open the steering column, but first he checked the sun visor, and a single key fell out. He caught it with his right hand.

"Saw it in a movie once," he said. He wondered why he talked to himself so much. No one cared what he had to say, he supposed.

As he started the truck, he checked to see if his new friend was in the back. He pressed down on the gas, and the two of them began making progress toward the target on the map as he smashed the side window out with his elbow and put his arm on the door.

"That's better," he said as he turned the radio on. There was no music, just people on the radio who were in panic mode and screaming about how terrible things were getting all over the city and there wasn't any help coming. The screams of the damned would have to do, he supposed it was better than nothing.

Once Dustin could look into the darkening sky as the power was going out around them, he could see jets in the distance. They were in combat with something. Dustin didn't want to see what it was.

Dustin drove down the street and turned a corner. He stopped some distance away from a rather impressive roadblock. A large number of troops and a tank to stop people from leaving.

Dustin thought about what to do next as he sat there staring at it and was soon aware that they must not have noticed him. It was then Sparky pushed his head into and through the glass behind him, breaking it, and rested his metallic head on his shoulder as if trying to help him think of a plan. Dustin didn't even notice the broken glass.

"You think we should give it a try?" he asked the metal cat. It agreed with what he was thinking somehow, even if it never said a word. "That's a terrible idea, but what the hell," he replied.

"Right, you should hold on to something," he said and slammed on the gas towards the roadblock. He stuck his left arm out the window and put his flamethrower on standby. It was all part of the plan, after all.

It wasn't long before the soldiers saw him coming down the road and got to their places, pointed their rifles, and started screaming "stop" at the speeding truck. Dustin didn't slow down.

He waited until the last second and spun his truck to the side in an instant. Halfway into the turn, he sent his flames at the soldiers in one wave.

The soldiers never got a chance to fire their weapons as they dived out of the way to avoid being burned to death. Sparky flinched at the sight of the fire as he lay down in the bed of the truck, claws dug into and through the metal. Dustin completed his maneuver and managed to regain control of the truck to drive through the flaming blockade with ease.

"That's going to be reported to someone who doesn't need to hear it," he said and looked at the rearview mirror to try and see if anyone was dead or not, but it was impossible to tell. "I'm sure everyone's fine," Dustin said and stepped on the gas.

Dustin justified this tactic on soldiers. They knew the job was dangerous when they took it, and he felt no remorse for killing anyone in uniform. As far as he was concerned, they were getting in the way and had no business dealing with this mess.

Sure, they were following orders, but he didn't care. His orders were far more important than anything they were doing. They were dying for their country. They would be called heroes no matter who killed them. And since the Squad didn't exist, they were killed by the enemy as far as anyone was concerned.

Dustin hated war, but when it came to the business of waging war, he was a professional. It was a job like any other.

The road had evidence of battle all over the place, and it forced him to pay attention now. Vehicles showed clear evidence of laser damage as they were cut in half. Whatever happened here didn't go well for the military. This was one battle he was glad he missed.

There was more going on here than an attack on the city. This had to be an inside job on some level, and when this was all over, he was going to make sure that this never happened again, somehow.

He had no idea what to expect up ahead but knew he wasn't going to like it.

## 39

Blake crawled away as best as he could, but the plane crash took the energy out of him, and standing was still difficult. He was looking for his rifle, and the fires spreading from the plane crash were making it easier to see in the dark.

"Where's my rifle?" he asked. At once, about ten feet in front of him, his gun was highlighted. He managed to pull himself halfway off the ground when a metal hand grabbed him by the back of the neck.

"You wear metal, but you are soft inside, soft and weak," the knight said with an angry electronic voice. Then it tossed him forward like an angry child flinging a toy into a wall. Blake crashed to the ground, and it was apparent that his enemy didn't see where his gun was. Blake wasted no time in grabbing the weapon, switching it to the explosive round setting as he rolled over and took aim.

"What's your point?" he asked and fired. The bullet stuck to its head and knocked it back. Then he set off the explosive, and the head was removed in a blast of flame and blue ooze in all directions.

The machine fell to its knees, face forward into the ground. Blake had no choice but to do that. For a second, there was silence. Maybe he was safe. That feeling died when he heard the sound of thunderous metal footsteps coming in his direction.

"Cloak," Blake said but watched as his armor flickered uselessly. It needed recharge, and that would take time. He wasn't even sure it would help against machines anyway. He stood up, ignoring the pain. He walked to see what the threat was, and up the hill from his first target was a line of eight, like the one he killed.

All of the knights held human weapons. Blake was sure they were ones that they collected since the invasion began, but why did they need them? It didn't make sense.

Blake wondered if the dead could be converted because he hadn't seen any dead people since this whole thing started. It was an interesting thought. One that he hoped wasn't real.

The eight saw him up the hill and opened fire. Blake knew that a direct attack wasn't possible, so he did the only thing open to him: he ran away. Blake had no taste for running away. "God-damned robots," he said, thankful they were slow.

Blake took advantage of his position and turned around to scan the area. From where he was, he could see his target, but not clear enough to know what it was. "Damn it," he said. He supposed even if he had a clear look, it wouldn't help much. The machines proved to be idiots. Once they got to where Blake was, they scanned the area and, as soon as they didn't see him, turned around and headed back.

He waited to make sure it wasn't a trap. As soon as it felt safe, he began to make his way towards the target.

He wasn't sure how long it took to move downhill while doing his best to not attract attention. Fear wasn't a factor. He was trying to keep the fight on his terms for as long as he could.

Blake wasn't sure if he was getting away with anything or if they were letting him get to where he needed to be to set a trap.

Either way, it didn't matter because he had a job to do.

It wasn't long before he could see the target and still, he had no idea what or who it was supposed to be. He could see a large glowing blue cylinder that was constantly shooting off bright blue arcs of power. Between each of the events, he could see something that looked human inside.

Blake looked around at the spread-out knights and each time one of these electric pulses discharged, the eyes of the enemy went brighter and dimmer right alongside it. He realized that he had no idea what to do next and considered his options.

He imagined two plans. The first one involved him crawling away a good distance, finding a nice spot and picking off the enemy one at a time. And then there was plan B. Blake, every once in a while, was a fan of plan B.

Blake took a deep breath and decided that now was a good time to explore the rest of his weapon's settings. Nothing was looking promising until he got down to the setting in his armor's visor menu that had the label emergency automatic fire. Blake couldn't fathom the idea of a fully automatic sniper rifle. This qualified as an emergency.

He selected it and his rifle made a slight click. He decided that there was no action like the direct kind and stood up.

"Hey, I'm over here," Blake said as he couldn't come up with anything else to say. In hindsight, he was wondering why he said anything at all. It was a bad habit he picked up from watching too much television over the years.

The machines turned in his direction. He squeezed the trigger. The kickback of the rapid fire knocked him off his feet. "Son of a Thursday," he said, shocked as he hit the ground and slid back a few feet. Blake pulled himself back up as fast as he could, braced himself, and tried it again.

He didn't bother aiming at all as he pointed in the general direction of the enemies and hoped for the best. The roar of his cannon was so loud that he was sure that without his armor he would have blown out his hearing.

He grit his teeth as he fought the extreme force. The nano system was pushed to its limit, keeping up with the rapid use of ammo from this assault. Blake turned his rifle on the knights as they walked out of the dark as fast as he could.

They fell to pieces before his eyes and their blue blood turned into a fine mist in the air. He hoped this was enough to keep them down for good, but optimism was dangerous.

The enemy barely had any time to react at first, but the ones farther away began to shoot back with their stolen weapons. Blake felt the bullets bounce off his armor but ignored them. He was confident that outlasting these things wouldn't be a problem.

One of the knights threw something that was flashing red. It caught Blake's attention just as it went over his head. Blake never had time to see what it was or try to run. It exploded with such a force that it knocked him off his feet, into the air, towards the enemy.

He let the trigger go as he fell through the air, hit the ground face first, and his weapon was knocked free, sliding away from him. Blake tried to stand up, but a metal foot slammed into his back, pressing him right back down into the ground.

"You've killed many of us, but that ends now," it said. Blake wondered when a machine cared about anything and when he missed that memo.

"Yeah, you think so? The way I see it, I'm just getting started," Blake replied as another one picked him up by the back of the neck with one arm. "We bring him to the judge," the one who was carrying him said, and they began to walk to the blue cylinder.

Blake had no idea what to expect as he was dropped in front of the blue cylinder and hit his knees. For some reason, he was expecting the thing to talk with some disembodied voice, but there was nothing.

The machines were in communication with the thing, maybe a mental link, he wasn't sure. There was no reason to wait around for a verdict and decided that he wouldn't get a better chance than now to do something.

He pointed his right arm and fired his zip line into the knight that brought him here, then sent an electrical charge through the line. The knight's systems overloaded, and it fell to its knees.

He retracted the line and stood up, having no idea what to do next. This escape plan wasn't thought out past this point.

Without thinking about it, he ran straight at the power source with as much speed as he could build in such a short distance. With his shoulder, he rammed the cylinder. To his surprise, the glass shattered into a million pieces, and he fell through to the other side as some kind of strange clear liquid exploded and covered Blake.

"What is this stuff and--" he stopped as he looked around. All of the machines in the area deactivated at the same time or got stunned. It was impossible to tell.

Then he noticed the woman that was laying there on the ground, still in the clothes she was taken in, and he had forgotten about that part when he rushed the power source like he did. "Damn it, I can't leave you here, I guess," he said and scanned her to make sure she was alive as he looked around for his rifle too.

Blake wanted to report in, but there was no telling who was listening in on the conversation, so he decided against it. It took a few seconds of looking to find his rifle in the hand of the enemy.

He walked over and pulled the weapon out of its grasp. His armor told him it was overheated and needed at least ten minutes of recovery time before it could be used again. He reattached his weapon to his back and walked over to the woman on the ground, hoping that she was still human on the inside.

His scans couldn't detect anything that was wrong, so he had no choice but to trust them for now. Not knowing what to do next, he picked her up and started to walk back to the city to find a place to hold up until the others reported in. He quickened his pace when from behind him, he thought he could hear the sounds of metal things coming back to life.

# 40

Wyatt was going as fast as he could push his bike. Racing the clock now was easy, traveling like this because there was no resistance along the way and the miles began to slide by in a hurry. He had a feeling that the way there was not going to be the same as the way back, as the way back was never easy.

There might not have been any resistance, but he felt that he was being watched by something, even if constant scans of his surroundings revealed nothing in the area. Wyatt's traveling time was nowhere as bad as he thought. He reached the city limits at last and came to a stop. This is where the target was supposed to be, but this is not what he was expecting.

This place looked okay, but it was dead quiet too. Maybe that was normal for this hour, maybe they hadn't heard of the invasion yet. He found that unlikely. If there was an enemy here, Wyatt didn't see or detect anything besides the target his armor had locked onto.

"This isn't good. I don't see anyone. Where did everyone go?" he asked himself to disrupt the oppressive silence as he pulled the bike to the side and killed the engine. This made it worse. He walked to the sidewalk and looked around, scanned everything but still there was nothing.

FLESH AND IRON

The whole place was a ghost town and that fact made it all the more unsettling. He needed a better look, so he found a building and in one jump made it to the roof. The view was better, but it didn't help. There was a wind blowing through the town, blowing papers around in various places but nothing else.

He couldn't even see the energy source. To his surprise, the second he jumped on the roof his armor lost track of it.

Wyatt was liking this less by the minute. Something was messing with him.

He walked to the edge and looked over it when a pair of eye beams slammed into the building under where he was standing. The force knocked him off his feet. It wasn't a direct hit, but the shock was enough to make him land on his back and he didn't bother sitting up.

It was a sniper attack and sitting up was going to get him killed even faster. He hated snipers and didn't even like Blake's style much. It was a pathetic way to do business.

This thing could have hit him the first time but didn't. What kind of a game was it playing, and since when did robots do stuff like that?

He scanned for anything but there were still no signs of life or movement anywhere near him. Wyatt knew how to deal with snipers, human ones anyway. This was his first encounter with a machine sniper. He had a plan and hoped that it would work. Trying anything was better than laying here waiting to die.

He rolled over and crawled to the other end of the roof. With his throwing knife, he carved out a chunk of the roof and threw it straight up. The lasers fired again and obliterated the target in a second. His thoughts were proven right, but the lasers moved so fast that it was impossible to tell what direction they came from. He knew he needed a new approach to this, but first, he had to get off this roof.

He crawled over to the opposite edge of the roof, turned over, and lowered himself feet first over a window. With one easy kick, he broke the glass and easily got inside. It was as empty and silent as everything else was here.

He walked to a window on the opposite side of the room and looked out as he slid his visor up and found out that he had relied on his armor too much, silently cursing himself out for being so dependent at the same time.

He could see the machines in the windows. They must have been suppressing their own energy so they would be invisible to detection. Wyatt had no idea what the truth was. It was as good a theory as any other.

From what he could see, they had every angle covered. They had lost the element of surprise, but it didn't matter anymore. He needed a new plan. His thoughts were broken when he could hear movement below him, the sound of metal footsteps.

Not wanting to waste any more time, he decided that seeing the enemy was better than guessing where they might be. He ventured out into the black hallway from the room to complete his mission or do something stupid, he wasn't sure yet.

He pulled out his blade and prepared to fight as the first came around the corner and saw it was like the others. A person infected with metal. A first stage monster was still a monster.

Wyatt lunged forward, clearing the hallway in one long jump and impaled the former human through the neck.

He was sure if the monster could scream in pain, it would have tried by now. It hit the floor, tiny sparks came from the wound along with it oozing the thick, black fluid. He couldn't kill them all. There wasn't enough time for this nor did he have the patience. He needed a new way to deal with the threat.

He had no time to think about it as another infected human turned the corner and paid no attention to the dead one on the floor. It was then Wyatt got an idea and jumped back from his new enemy. It fired at him with those same blue eye beams as before. Wyatt deflected the beams into the wall and as he hoped, he watched as it started a fire.

The flame was small, but it was spreading across the wall and up. Wyatt didn't know how much these things wanted to live or not, but there was no telling how many there were inside the building. It was a better choice to burn the whole thing down. With no power or help coming, he was sure this building would go up fast and all he had to do was avoid the enemies.

He turned a corner and broke through a thick door without hesitation to another room. He ran for the window without looking at what was outside first, jumped through it, and landed on the street. Without wasting any time, he took off running. It looked to be some kind of a restaurant. He slipped inside and disappeared.

Wyatt didn't need to wait long as he saw the smoke begin to pour out of the windows. The fire was doing its job. The machines in the building were fleeing but not fast enough. With any luck, the fire would take them all. He was hoping that would happen but didn't depend on it.

The snipers on the other side of the building saw the fire as an attack and left their posts too. Moving to the ground to hunt for the attacker.

The ones in the building were only first stage infected but the snipers were completely transformed into knights and posed more of a threat. There was no better time than now to say hello, so he tightened his grip on his blade as he walked out of his hiding place to face his enemies.

"I suppose you don't like the idea of coming out to face me like the men or women you once were on even ground. Well, that's too bad. Get ready to die like the cowards you are," he said, getting their attention.

He then took the sword in both hands and took a fighting stance. There were sixteen of the things. They stood there with no emotion in their hollow eyes. The blue burning lights were visible, and they were all looking in his direction.

Wyatt prepared to deal with them all in one shot like he did last time, but when they fired their eye beams, they did not shoot at him. Instead, each of them began to fire at different points. There was no way Wyatt could block them all at once, and he was hit several times as he tried avoiding the attacks.

Searing pain coursed through his body upon impact. These beams sliced through various pieces of his armor and right into his flesh. If he fell now, he knew he would die, so he ignored the pain as best as he could and decided it was better to run away as he realized this plan was a failure.

Wyatt hated to run away from anyone or anything, ever. Those beams were vicious, and the enemy was evolving each time he faced them. The same trick wouldn't work again.

He stopped running and collapsed against a wall in pain. He heard the stomping feet of the metal things around the corner. They were relentless. "Why am I running away? Am I scared of these things? No, that can't be right."

He pushed off the wall and turned around, holding the blade with both hands, and stepped from behind the corner.

He looked at them as they continued their death march. Wyatt smiled under his helmet for a brief second and charged the enemy as fast as he could.

He jumped into the air and attacked the one closest. The blade came down and cleaved the head in half. It was a first-stage infected, and the blade met little resistance. There was no stopping this momentum as he pulled the blade out and ran the tip across the neck of the one next to it.

It fell. Black fluid running onto the ground made him take pause. He was used to red, not black. As he did this, one of them grabbed his sword arm and pulled it back. They were much stronger than they looked.

"Damn it, let go," Wyatt said as he twisted his arm free, spun around, and with one swing of his blade, he cut the former human in half. The pieces fell to the ground, and the spray covered him in that black ooze.

Another one took advantage of the pause and slammed its fist into Wyatt's face. The impact knocked him across the street, into a streetlight, and he took the pole down with him. It crashed at the same time he did.

Wyatt groaned.

This was no time to be stunned, so he pulled himself up and stumbled out of the way of a beam attack. Something exploded behind him. This wasn't working either, and he needed a better plan.

"Suggestions?"

"Use your throwing knives to even the odds," his armor replied. He wasn't expecting anything to respond.

"I have them?" he asked while barely avoiding four more beams.

"Yes, you do," the armor replied, and there was a small click where a belt might have been. Three blades emerged on each side of his waist.

"Thank you." At once, he drew them, three in each hand between his fingers.

He leapt into the air and threw all of his throwing knives at the horde. Three of the lesser machines fell as the blades sunk into their skulls. The other three had much thicker armor, and the blades bounced off.

Needing this encounter to come to an end, he ran in a half circle around the group as they shot at him. Wyatt was leaving a swath of destruction in his wake. Wyatt couldn't believe how fast he was moving right now.

He felt the armor pull at his joints, and they felt like they were going to tear to pieces.

The mechanical things didn't know how to handle something so fast besides to shoot at it. The enemy was programmed to fight humans.

"What is it, why is the target moving so fast?" one of the knights asked, and Wyatt couldn't help but smile at the distress he was causing to a machine of all things.

Wyatt didn't feel human anymore, not entirely. More like a demon possessed with the power of speed itself as he sliced through the flesh-infected steel at a rapid pace. Wyatt was lost in the power and the thrill. He watched as his blade cut through an arm as if it were made out of butter. The blue blood came, but it was in slow motion.

He couldn't help but smile. No longer himself, more so he felt as if he were a living god of velocity that was unstoppable. He couldn't believe that he was this fast.

The enemy, any enemy, would fall before him now, and nobody could stand against this power. He wondered why he was even on a team at all. With this kind of power, he wouldn't need anybody else.

He decided that this would be the last mission he'd ever go on as a member of the Squad. He'd take the armor for himself, use it against anyone who dared challenge him. They'd be cut into pieces.

As he plunged the blade into the heart of the last machine, he watched the life fade from its blue eyes. Then he cut its head off to make sure it wouldn't stand back up. He was surrounded by dismembered bodies all in a pool of their own black and thick blue blood.

He waved his hands and the throwing knives returned with a magnetic pull on instinct. He caught them and put them back on his belt in a second.

It was too easy. Everything was so slow. He didn't remember feeling like this before, but something had changed, and he liked it.

His armor still wasn't detecting the original target, but he didn't care. With this speed, he could search the whole area in record time, but something else was eating at him now. He wanted more, so much more to test his power.

He was looking for a challenge.

Here was a town with nobody in it, and it was so frustrating. Was this all part of the plan they had, the machines, or someone else maybe? He wasn't sure. What made it all worse were the various Christmas decorations hanging in various places, swaying in the breeze.

It made everything feel even more abandoned. The feeling was oppressive. It was strange how festive things without people had the opposite effect.

All of this was a ploy to ruin his mind. He couldn't think of anything worse. Maybe it was a trap. No, he had to get a hold of himself. He hadn't looked in the right places yet, that was all. Wyatt's mind began to race now that he wasn't moving.

He eventually would find what he was looking for, and when that happened, there was going to be no saving anything standing in his way.

Then the black started to seep in through his visor. The night was invading, creeping in from all directions like a living slime.

Without thinking, he tried to wipe it off, but it held on. He fell to his knees in a panic, his heart pounding in his ears, the sound of rushing blood was unbearable. Wyatt closed his eyes and began counting.

"What in the hell is wrong with me?" he asked and tried to calm his mind down. "In and out, breathe," he said. Slowly the panic subsided. His mind and heart slowed down too. The madness was leaving, and when he opened his eyes, the night was outside where it belonged.

"I need to fight the right battle. I need to find the right target," he said, clearing his head of the insanity at least for now.

"Do another scan. Scan for energy signals that don't belong to this grid. Find everything," Wyatt said and waited.

"Energy sources detected, alien to the grid, locating now," it said. He smiled. "Just had to know what to ask for and how," he said, standing up, inspecting the damage to his armor and seeing it wasn't too bad after all. "Right, I have an appointment to keep."

Wyatt started to walk to the target. Running might have made him slip back into the darkness, and that was one thing he didn't need.

He moved in the direction his armor gave him. For a few minutes, like before, everything was dead. To his amazement, and maybe some horror, he discovered the target was the Diamond Bar High School. The sign out front said it was established in 1982. That must have been ancient to the kids who went here now.

"What?" He tried to figure out what was going on. He hoped none of the kids were here. With any luck, everyone was safe.

He had to believe in delusions like that to keep sane. Even if he thought things were under control, one mistake meant disaster.

Wyatt spied on the scene from a safe distance. The machines were surrounding a blue cylinder that was discharging arcs of power in a rhythmic pattern in front of the school. They were worshiping it as some kind of God. It appeared to be the life source for them.

Wyatt looked at it, and inside he could barely see the outline of what looked like a kid when the discharge was at its brightest.

It could have been a trick of the light, too. If this was what he was seeing, it should have been unforgivable by anyone's standards. He narrowed his eyes and channeled his armor's full speed. The plan was simple now. This time he'd clear his mind and remain focused.

He jumped from the dark and took them all by surprise. Wyatt stabbed one in the back. The tip of his sword slammed into the ground as he impaled the machine and knocked it over. It got the attention of the others.

"I guess church is over," Wyatt said as they stood up and turned towards him.

Wyatt was outnumbered, but they were outmatched. He didn't care how many there were. He would take them all on one at a time or all at once. He was ready to go, but they didn't move. He wasn't sure what made him more nervous. A horde of attacking robots or ones that stared at him.

"Well, aren't you impressive, taking down all of my friends?

After all, you are quick on your feet. I've been watching you, Syndicate dog. Your services are no longer required," something said as it moved out of the dark and faced him.

It was a slender machine. It had dried blood on its claws and the eyes glowed dark green. It had the shape of a minotaur that hadn't eaten in decades. It was covered in purple and gold paint, too. Wyatt didn't understand why.

"You got a little, uh, wild with the makeup?" he asked and took a step forward. The minotaur looked down. "Yeah, I killed a few stragglers hiding in the art room. Apparently, the school's colors are purple and gold. There was an accident. I'm sure some more red will make it all come together," the thing replied.

"I doubt it," Wyatt replied. The minotaur took another step. "I guess we'll just have to find out."

Wyatt waited a second too long, and the mechanical minotaur ran at Wyatt so fast it turned into a purple and gold blur. "Son of a bitch," Wyatt said, getting the wind knocked out of him as he was torn off the ground. The thing lifted him with one hand and proceeded to drive Wyatt into the pavement and through it.

"I'm no dog," Wyatt managed to say, still trying to get a handle on his situation.

"I don't care," it replied in its mechanical voice. Wyatt stretched his left arm out above his head and fired his zipline. It hooked onto something, and as the metal fist came down again, Wyatt was dragged away, carving a path through the pavement in a shower of sparks.

Wyatt was impressed. There was a chance to test his new power. He pulled himself out of the rubble. The bull was already staring at him.

He held his blade tight and ran forward, closing the distance in two seconds. He leapt into the air and swung his blade, and the edge scraped along the steel face as it ducked and put its fist into Wyatt's stomach, pushing him back into the air. The minotaur spun around and kicked him to send Wyatt back into the ground.

"You are so slow. Maybe I should let you get a free shot just to make you feel better?" it asked in a mocking tone as it held Wyatt down with a foot on his chest.

"What are you supposed to be, anyway?" Wyatt asked. The minotaur tilted its head in confusion.

"Me, I guess I wasn't given a name. I should have a name," it replied as Wyatt looked for a way out. "Well, a name would be good, you know, for birthday parties," Wyatt said as the pressure increased.

"I suppose you're right. I'll be Chris," the machine said, and Wyatt stopped looking for a way out. "Chris, really? Yeah, you look more like a Sprocket to me. It matches your weird dark green glowing eyes," Wyatt said, and the two of them drifted off into a strange silence.

"What's a sprocket?" the minotaur asked. Wyatt had no idea, he half remembered it from an old cartoon when he was a kid.

Wyatt used the distraction to put his left fist into the ankle of the machine hard enough to make it lose its balance and stumble to the side. Wasting no time to take advantage, he got back to his feet. He lunged forward and put the end of the sword at Sprocket's head, right between those green eyes.

It reacted by reaching out and catching the blade, putting it between the palms and stopping it. Then, without pausing, it twisted the blade to the right and brought the rest of its body up to kick Wyatt in the face with more force than he expected.

This caused Wyatt to let go of his blade and fall back to the ground on his back. "What the hell is the deal with all the damn kicking?" Wyatt said, stumbling away, shaking his head to regain his senses.

The minotaur spun the blade around and grabbed it with its oversized hand, making the whole sword seem tiny in comparison. With Hell Razor's blade in its hands, Sprocket walked towards Wyatt while he was still dazed.

"Nice piece of metal you have here. Too bad you can't use it. Oh wait, I suppose you are having trouble hearing with your head ringing like a bell, right?" Sprocket said with a fair amount of sarcasm for a machine. He swung the blade back and forth a couple of times before throwing it away. It sunk halfway into the ground on impact.

Some bull headed thing wasn't going to get the best of him, not today at least. "I don't need a sword to beat you," he said, the anger rising in him. The minotaur blitzed, horns first. It was too fast to avoid. Wyatt put his hands up and grabbed the horns. There was no chance to stop it. He dug his feet in and slid through the pavement.

Wyatt thought his arms were about to break along with his armor. With no other choice, he jumped up and over the metal beast, landing on its back. "Get off me," Sprocket said and came to a stop. Wyatt tried to twist the head to the side but managed to twist the horns a couple of inches. Sprocket grabbed Wyatt's wrists and tossed him through a car in the parking lot. The thing exploded as he tore through it. "No, black one, that's not going to work either."

Wyatt winced in pain, thankful he made his way through the fire and did not get stuck in it. For all this new armor and power, he felt useless now. "God damned Protobots," Wyatt said, rolling away to stand up. Without missing a beat, he rushed back into the fight as fast as he could. He threw his left fist, and the minotaur raised its arm to block it.

Wyatt heard his fingers crack the second he hit the steel. Even on the defense, it was a losing battle. He drew his fist back. The throbbing pain was fading already, but he realized there was nothing he could do here. "Usually in a boss fight, the boss sends in the grunts to fight. Why are all of them standing there watching?" he asked, trying to buy time.

"I don't need help to kill you."

Wyatt didn't understand how this thing was so powerful. He needed a new approach, something that didn't end with him getting kicked in the head every ten seconds or breaking his own bones trying to fight. Now was no time to be fancy.

"You know, Chris, I never thought I'd lose to a robot. You're good, and that almost makes me sorry for what I am about to do," Wyatt said.

Sprocket tilted his head and looked at him. "What do you mean sorry?" he asked Wyatt and was confused. There was nothing he could do in this situation. "Almost sorry," Wyatt said as he pulled out one of his throwing knives, and with all his power, he threw the blade at the power source.

It caught the blade in its right hand as if it were picking a flower from a garden. As soon as the minotaur was distracted, he threw a second one. It shot through the glass as if it were a bullet, and the structure shattered.

The body of a kid slid out as the strange liquid poured onto the ground. The power source was dead. Wyatt looked over at his enemy, and it had powered down and looked as if it were a purple and gold statue in a fighting pose and always had been. "The school can use you as a mascot if we live through this, Sprocket," he said and turned towards something more interesting.

Wyatt walked over to the kid who now had a knife stuck in his shoulder. He was no more than ten years old and still alive but bleeding. How he wasn't dead was a mystery. "Weird," Wyatt said, confused.

"This is Wyatt, mission accomplished. I think. If you can hear me, I'm heading back to the Tower, and I am bringing company too, I guess." Wyatt walked over to his sword, pulled it from the road, and stuck the end of it into the fire.

He waited until the sword was glowing hot. It didn't take too long. Wyatt found it weird how the blade always got that hot so fast. It was almost supernatural.

He pulled the sword out of the fire and walked to the victim. Not sure what to do about the situation, he thought about it for a second then knelt down. "Sorry," he said and pulled out the knife and put the hot blade on the wound at the same time. As far as he could tell, it worked. "There. That should do the trick," he said. The wound wasn't bleeding anymore, but it still looked ugly.

He looked back to Chris, still frozen. In the quiet, beyond the crackling of the flames, he could hear a distant, faint voice.

Wyatt looked around but saw no one nearby, and at once had a terrible thought as he walked to the machines and got closer. He realized that the voice was coming from inside the armor, a human voice trapped inside.

Wyatt's eyes widened, and he rushed to it. "Hey, are you alive in here?" he asked and then waited. "How come I can't see, where am I?" the weak voice asked from inside the armor. Wyatt's eyes widened, and at once he pulled his sword and stabbed through the armor on the left side as far away from the middle as he could to make an opening. He almost wondered why he couldn't do this before.

The lack of a cry of pain or blood was a good sign. He put his sword down and took the opening in both hands to pry the thing apart. For a few seconds, all was going well when he retracted as the firelight revealed the horror.

There was a man here, what was left of him anyway. His body was filled with metal and wires. The pale white flesh melded in with the organic black steel, and he recoiled on instinct.

"Oh, it's still you. I thought I killed you, sorry about that. I get to see glimpses," the man's bloodshot eyes turned to Wyatt, and his voice was racked with pain. "I was put into one of those booths hours ago. I've done the same to many, well, I watched anyway," he said and tried to look away. "Don't worry, I can get you out of here and—" Wyatt was cut off.

"No, you can't save me. I saw you with the blade. You know what you have to do. I can feel this machine coming back to life. Without me, it's not coming back," the man said and closed his eyes. "Sorry about this," Wyatt said as he drew his sword, and with one quick movement, impaled the man through the chest, ending his life.

He pulled his blade out, then picked up a flaming piece of debris and tossed it into the opening. The black coating on the metal burned and was hot enough to make him back off.

Then he noticed it. Screaming, a chorus of muffled screaming. "I can't breathe, help, I can't see," the voices cried out in desperation. He looked at the metal minions, still frozen in place. The people in the knights were still alive.

Wyatt knew there was nothing he could do for them. He also knew that they could be stuck in those bodies for as long as they remained. "Damn it."

His wrath turned on the steel things. One by one, he removed their heads, ending the screaming, the begging and pleading, until it was all quiet. Wyatt took a deep breath and knew that he had to keep moving. There'd be time to think about everything later, maybe.

He put his blade away and walked to the kid. "You poor bastard," Wyatt said and picked him up, realizing that he was about twenty-seven miles away from where he needed to be. Now he had a kid to take with him, or at least part of the way until he found somewhere safe, somewhere that wasn't here at least.

"I hate escort missions," Wyatt said and started to walk back, trying to figure out a way to tie the kid to the bike he left behind to make this easier.

# 41

Josh walked with the leader deeper into the scrap metal fortress as semi-organic eyes watched his every move from the dark and the tops of the surrounding high walls. "We don't want to die, much like you, I suppose. For the new to come into the world, obviously, the old one must be removed," the red cloaked leader said as they walked on.

"Yes, but who's to say when humanity's time is up?" Josh asked, trying to be civil despite the nature of the conversation.

"They created us. They sealed their own fate when they did. Sure, you will try and stop us, but in the end, we will win the fight. Just as mammals defeated the reptiles, machines will defeat humanity and replace them," it said and pushed the door open with one hand.

This door was four feet thick, made from metal, and eight feet high, and this did not escape Josh's notice as it moved with nearly no effort. Inside was the power source, a bright blue cylinder glowing with power in a strange rhythm. Josh could see the outline of a female inside as it got brighter.

Josh narrowed his eyes but didn't clench his fists or show any signs of outward anger to avoid a metallic blitz for as long as he could.

"Do you see? Humans have their purpose. This one and four others were discovered to have special energies to help keep us alive. We do not wish for them to be with us here. The sight of them revolts us, as you do. In order to live, we must keep this one here until the sun sets tomorrow."

Josh understood the struggle to survive and how hard it was sometimes. He had been a victim of this battle all his life, and he could sympathize, but at the same time, the ones they were going to kill were humanity, and he couldn't allow this to continue because apparently, that was the side he was on.

Even if he thought that humanity deserved an eradication event, it should be quick, not like this.

"I can't stand by and let this happen. I guess I am going to have to stop you," he said but not that convincingly. The leader's head looked at the ground.

"I figured you might say that. The things you and your team have been killing are but children, you know? Just starting out in life, attacking anything with a gun, and like all life forms, seek to increase our numbers. My hope was that someday humans and machines might co-exist. I don't think this is possible. People have never been too good at tolerance according to the historical records." Josh didn't feel good about what he had to do next.

"I will make this easy on you. You and I will fight, of course. If I win, you leave and fail your mission, but I won't kill you if you give up. If you win, the power source is yours," the leader said and looked at him. Josh shrugged.

"It's the fairest deal I'll get today," he said, knowing he had no choice but to win this contest and hoped that it was honorable. The memory of the door being pushed open with one hand did not escape him.

"Go outside and wait. You will not be harmed. I will be with you shortly." Josh nodded and turned to walk out the way he came, thinking that this had to be the strangest encounter he had ever had.

Josh made his way back down the same path towards the

outside, ready for any kind of surprise attack, but about halfway back he was sure that if they were going to attack, they would have already.

Within minutes, he was back outside and walked a few steps down the road to find a good waiting spot. The wait was not a long one. The leader must have been right behind him. It scared him a little that he didn't notice such a thing so close. He pushed all that out of his mind. Now was the time to focus.

"They have orders not to get in the way no matter what happens," it said as he took off his cloak and threw it to the door behind him. It landed on one of the random spikes. "You seem to be honorable, how did you get like this?" Josh asked, figuring anyone would have wondered the same thing.

"I looked it up on something called Google what it meant to be a hero. I liked what it said, so I stuck with it." Josh almost laughed and was going to ask how a machine liked anything, but now it was obvious.

"Alright, whenever you're ready," Josh said and prepared himself. He had no idea what to expect. The leader clenched his steel fists, and his body began to shift places, and it became clear that it was growing.

"Molecular control over the steel in my body allows me to achieve maximum potential. I am sorry, but for my world and people to survive, you can't win. I will do anything it takes," it said and grew to be thirteen feet tall. It was a steel colossus. Josh was now looking up at his opponent and crossed his arms.

"You know, this isn't fair," he said and took a step back. "Maybe not fair, but I suspected you found my other form to be too weak for a worthy challenge." Josh sighed because that wasn't what he was thinking.

"Okay, but this big is a bit much, don't you think?"

The leader considered this question. "No," it said and put the giant right fist into the ground with enough power to create a shockwave that knocked Josh off his feet and to the ground, but as soon as he did, Josh pointed his arms at the giant and opened fire.

The leader took the shots and was pushed back a little, blocking his face with his hands on instinct. The bullets were meant for fleshy opponents, not ones made out of metal that could control their bodies to the point of growing six extra feet. It was a distraction.

Josh took advantage of the distraction and knew his physical power was going to be more useful here than his weapons. He didn't know how he was going to beat this one, but he wouldn't stop trying. He couldn't afford to stop.

He stood up and lunged and put both of his fists into the machine's chest as fast as he could. The impact made the leader go off balance but not fall over. Josh was too close, and he knew it as it grabbed hold with its immense left hand.

It spun him around, smashed him into the black wall of the fortress with a great amount of force as if he were nothing more than a toy, and held him there.

Josh felt that through his armor, and the systems were telling him that impact alone was near the limits of his endurance.

He smashed both of his hands down onto the wrist of the thing, and it was enough force to make him fall to the ground. Josh landed on his feet and sprinted forward again using the wall as momentum. It tried to catch him but was too slow.

Josh avoided the grab attempt and, after that, he stepped to the left and kicked the machine's right leg out from under it with enough force to send the leader to the ground.

Josh rushed to take the advantage, but as he did, the giant left hand rose up and swatted him away with ease and with so much force he was thrown into the air and flew twenty feet before he hit the hard pavement with enough force to break through it.

Josh was still reeling from the attack when he heard the familiar scraping of his enemy getting up in the distance. His armor was telling him to run, but if he listened to that—well, there was no way he could listen to that now.

He forced himself to stand back up through the pain only to see the giant walking toward him.

"I am starting to not like you," Josh said to his enemy but had no time to think. Twenty feet was nothing to this giant, and the distance was covered in seconds.

It attempted to crush Josh, but at the last minute, he ducked the punch, moved in for the attack, and swung once with his left fist and slammed into the side. Then he followed up with a right jab.

This time the metal exoskeleton was dented. It was progress but not nearly enough to matter. He didn't want to stay close to it because to do that was to invite disaster. He tried to back away, but he was not fast enough as the leader used the back of its metal hand and threw him back into the shattered body of a burned out car. Josh didn't get up from this attack.

The leader was walking over to deliver the finishing blow to end this. "I can't let you win," the leader bellowed out in his metal voice. "Yeah, right back at you, metalhead," Josh replied with ever-growing rage mixed with pain.

The leader decided that it was time to end the battle. He stood over him and was proceeding to step on Josh like the bug he was.

Josh waited for the right time, then tightened his grip on the twisted body of the car and swung the left half into the machine with enough force to knock it back and into the earth.

"How do you like it?" Josh asked and proceeded to tear the rear axle from the car, throwing the rest away.

The second the leader landed on the ground, he moved to the top of the body and used that axle as a bat against the side of the leader's head. Again and again, Josh smashed the axle into its face, and with every attack, the leader's face was caved in a little more. It was unrelenting as it was vicious.

The next attack came, and the immense right hand grabbed the bent axle and stopped Josh in mid-swing.

The other hand came as the metal body twisted around and

blasted its fist into Josh's head, and he went flying again back into the dark. He was outmatched in this battle, and he knew it, but he wouldn't give up. Josh forced himself up once again despite it being hard to stand.

"Why don't you stay down, human? You can't beat me, and you know it," it said. "Maybe I can't, but it doesn't matter. You'll have to kill me to keep me down. There is no way I can let you do this," Josh replied, hoping it sounded as good as he thought. Because of the pain he was in, it was hard to tell.

The leader stood straight up and walked towards him. "You are impressive for a person. I don't want to kill you," the machine stopped walking.

Josh was ready for about anything, but not this. The eyes of the leader shifted a little.

"Maybe there is hope for your race yet. You go in and get what you came for. When you do, it'll shut us all down for a time. I'll hold the others back while you go," it said, and Josh shook his head.

"Why?" It was the only thing he could think of to ask. "I don't know. Maybe I like you because you're not dead yet. Maybe it's because I know that the machines are a bad substitute for humanity in the long run. Maybe it's the last remains of the human inside of me screaming for mercy. Let's do this before I change my mind," it said, and Josh didn't dare say anything about the sudden change.

"Alright, let's do it. You go first. I need a couple of minutes to recover. You hit hard," Josh said and shook his head, His healing factor was already kicking in, but it never worked fast enough when he needed it. "We go together, move it."

Josh and his former enemy walked side by side down the broken road. "So, you have a name?" Josh asked but never took his eyes off the fortress.

"I've always found the name David to be a good one," it said, and Josh almost laughed but decided against it. "It's a good name. I'm Josh, the poor bastard that signed up for this job," he replied.

"Oh, you might be small, but I think you have a great destiny ahead of you after all this is over," David said, and Josh looked up at his new ally.

"I'm not little, you're really big. As for destiny, let's try to make it through today," Josh said, but the trip to the fortress was a short one, and the new alliance was not a surprise to any of the machines inside as they didn't hide their approach.

"You ready?" Josh asked. "As I ever could be." The two of them stopped at the door.

David opened the jagged black gates with ease with his hands, and the machines that once restrained their attack realized that something was wrong.

"Go, now," the leader said, and from his black eyes came a stream of white energy that crashed into and pushed them back into the walls, and away from the entrance. Josh had to turn his head due to the sheer intensity.

"Why didn't you use that against me?" Josh asked, surprised as the light died down. "I could have, but it wouldn't have been fair. Now go," David said, and he didn't need to be told twice. He almost wondered if this wasn't the plan all along. There wasn't any time to think about it now.

Josh took off running down the path. The mostly human machines were jumping off the walls, trying to stop him, but he was avoiding them. They were slower to react. Far less advanced than the leader was.

One of the infected people landed in front of him. Without a second thought, Josh vaporized its head into blue mist with a burst of minigun fire. The body fell to the ground, its hands still clutching desperately into the air. He had to keep moving.

White flashes from behind told him the fight must have been going well. He turned a corner and stopped in his tracks as he saw six of the knights. "Damn it," he said and prepared to fight all of them at once. He pointed his dual cannons at them as they began to move in his direction.

A great steel hand latched onto Josh's shoulder. "No time to fight, the horde is coming," the leader said. As the blue eyes lit up, David threw him up and over the knights with ease. He landed on the metal ground behind the six of them. On his feet, the impact sent shockwaves of pain, but there was no time for that.

Josh took off running as fast as he could to the power source.

He made it to the gates and pressed on them, but they didn't move. It was then he remembered they opened up from the inside. He punched the metal as hard as he could. The bones in his hand broke, and the pain shot up his arm. He ignored it. There wasn't time for suffering.

He used the dent he made for leverage. The heavy metal doors began to open at last. He felt like he was going to tear every muscle in his arms doing it. Without the armor, this would have been impossible. The second he got them open, he remembered he had a zipline that might have made this whole experience easier.

He walked to the glowing cylinder and slammed his fist into the surface of the thing, but it didn't break. "Damn you, break already."

He punched the surface again and again. On the fourth, the thing let loose a powerful electric arc, brilliant blue and blinding being this close, but the container shattered.

It was now he noticed everything went silent outside. He looked and saw that person. She was still alive but sleeping. He hoped it wasn't a coma or anything like that.

He moved over to her. She couldn't have been more than seventeen years old, dressed in the clothes she was taken in. She was covered in the clear slime. He debated on leaving her there in his head, but that thought lasted a few seconds as he decided it was better to take her somewhere else.

She was special for a reason and he couldn't risk the enemy

getting their hands on this one again. "Why couldn't you be dead already? That would have made this easier," he said and picked her up.

He walked out of the room and saw the machines in various stages of transformation lying on the ground. He also heard faint screaming coming from every direction.

His giant ally was motionless as well, and Josh half expected him to wake up and have some kind of alternate power source, but nothing happened.

Not wanting to stay here anymore, he took his rescued victim, who was somehow still alive, and began to make his way out of the steel fortress into the night and had no idea where he was going to go from here.

# 42

Dustin could see the battle lines well and, somehow, he ended up on the wrong side. The firepower of the Army had been aimed at him. Neither he nor Sparky approved of this situation. Parked behind a building wasn't the best place to be, but for now it was safe.

Dustin could see how this was going to get worse. At least it explained why the trip here was so dead. He was following the advance of the machines the entire way.

"So damn close, too," he said with a sigh. He wondered that maybe, if he waited long enough, all the military forces would either retreat or die. Either way, it'd make his job easier.

For now, he'd listen to the sounds of battle and watch the vast black ocean in the distance. It wasn't the worst way to spend the time. All he was missing was a bottle and maybe some depressing Christmas music. He looked over to the metal cat and saw that something had its attention. Its eyes were focused on something. "What's the matter?" he asked.

A few seconds later, his scanners started going crazy as they detected the approach of something from the water. "Oh," he answered himself. There was nothing he could do but watch to see what was going to happen next. He decided he could at least get a better look. He got out of the truck and moved to the edge of the building to see around the corner.

Then from the darkness of the sea, the sound of boiling water came with the appearance of a vast and bright beam of blue-white light. It came from the sea and slammed into the American forces. Whatever the reason, they never saw it coming, and everything that beam touched was vaporized on contact.

The heat alone from this deadly light was enough to make things combust into flames by being close. It was a terrible sight to see, and Dustin almost looked away.

The tanks were melted as if they were made out of the wax of a cheap candle. The battle had, for a few seconds at least, been stopped as a large swath of destruction was cut through the American forces, leaving behind death and confusion.

The machines on the opposite side even appeared to show some kind of pity for them and stopped shooting. "My god," Dustin said, almost smiling. He'd never seen anything so powerful. All he could think about right now was that he needed to get whatever that was for himself.

Almost after the attack, the survivors turned their cannons to the sea and opened fire on the unseen enemy in an attempt to destroy it. However, the shells made the water explode and churn. There was no sign they were hitting anything at all. "Idiots."

Dustin's scanners also went dead as the new enemy disappeared. From somewhere far in the distance, mortar shells were landing into the ranks of the enemy, but they were getting too close to Dustin's spot for comfort as the shockwaves of the explosion were shaking his truck now.

"Well, Sparky. I guess it's time to get to work," he said and put his left hand on the metal cat's head. Then he looked at the truck. "Don't get blown up, please."

Dustin never did like all this sneaking around and hiding. He thought back to a time in his past when he was drunk and took on a snowbank. Sure, he lost, but that was a time long ago. Still, the fact remained that he took the direct approach no matter when or where the enemy would show up.

He was going to try and sneak through the ranks of the enemy and hoped that he wouldn't be noticed. At the same time, he tried to avoid being hit by any stray tank fire. He supposed that tank fire would put an end to his mission in a spectacular fashion.

He looked down at the metal cat. "Are you ready to do something stupid?" Sparky narrowed its eyes. "Good, let's get this over with." He took a deep breath and began to walk towards the machines in the distance.

The sight was surreal, and he expected the two forces to charge one another at any time. As he walked closer, he could see no reason why the machines didn't do it.

Was there more to this plan, or were they defending the target he was trying to get to and didn't dare leave their post? He had no idea and didn't care.

Dustin moved into the enemy's camp. None of them were interested in him as he moved through the bulk of the enemy.

Then a sudden and terrible noise got his attention. The metal cat leapt forward and sunk its teeth into a passing metal-infected human that had gotten too close, killing it, the blue and red blood spilled on the ground.

Sparky proceeded to drag it back to Dustin's feet. It dropped the body there and put one metal paw on it. The cat then looked at him and looked like it was smiling, proud too. Dustin wanted to disappear.

"Good kitty, but why did you have to do that now? This was a mistake, Sparky," Dustin said and at once felt the air around him change. He liked the cat, but he couldn't tell if it was because it learned to like him, or it reminded him of himself in so many ways. Then he couldn't decide if this reasoning was a good or bad thing after all because for most of this night he felt as if he was losing his mind and everything began to feel less real and more like some kind of illusion he was trapped in.

A city filled with infectious machines, power armor, and a metal cat at his side that could fly. It was all beginning to push the limits of madness he was willing to believe. In the end, it didn't matter what was real and what was insanity. He expected to wake up at any second, probably to learn he's been in Oz this whole time and there was a witch out there that needed another bucket of water. Dustin hated witches, they were always so messy.

His thoughts snapped back to the illusion he was currently in.

The killing of one attracted the attention of the rest of them, and soon he found himself the center of hostile intentions as once uncaring knights turned their burning blue eyes in his direction.

"Uh, the cat did it," Dustin said with a shrug. The whole thing was awkward.

Sparky didn't mind when it came to taking the credit for the kill as it narrowed its eyes at the same time. Dustin had little time to react, and he jumped to the left and put both hands on a knight and used it as a projectile to make some distance between himself and his enemies.

"Now I know how it must feel when you fail one of those stupid stealth missions in a game," he said as his makeshift weapon smashed into three infected people, knocking them over.

Dustin took the chance and ran through the opening he made as soon as he could to get away. All of this took a few seconds. He didn't want to get hit in the back with any lasers. He also didn't wait for Sparky, he was sure it'd be fine.

Dustin wasted no time in smashing through the wall of another building to find a little bit of cover, but staying here was not an option. Sparky came through the opening right behind him, followed by the rhythmic metal footsteps of the enemy who were not far behind. Dustin knew he was in trouble.

"Next time, cat, you need to wait for the signal. No random

killings, bad Sparky," Sparky looked at him and blinked twice in confusion. "Great, the cat is as dumb as I am," Dustin said before realizing what he said and decided not to worry about it.

Now he had a choice to make, the oldest choice in the world. He had to decide if he wanted to run or fight. He took a deep breath and decided that escape wasn't an option. There was no telling what was waiting for him, and he didn't want to run with nowhere to go.

He turned towards the opening and prepared his flamethrowers, pointed them at the opening. All he had to do now is wait, and the wait wasn't a long one. The silver knights appeared around the corner, and he didn't hesitate.

He unleashed his fire and watched as they kept walking, unaffected by the bright orange flames.

"Heat is not effective, impostor. We can withstand far greater temperatures," one of them said. He wondered if they hadn't said anything if he would have figured it out on his own before it was too late.

Dustin's armor was a walking weapon from what he could tell. He needed to try something else. "Let's see here, what I can do with this," he said as he flipped through the seemingly endless options on his internal menu, but in his distraction, a metal hand reached through the fire and grabbed him by the neck, lifted him up off the ground, killing the fire.

The pressure around his neck increased so fast he could feel it through his armor and warning indicators began to tell him stuff he already knew. "Hey, this one seems nice," he said. His weapon made an odd sound like it was rebooting when the knight smashed his head through a support pillar burying them both in rubble.

He had no idea why the machine didn't kill him outright. It was hard to think while your head was ringing like a bell. Maybe it was the human influence on the inside. He didn't know and didn't care. He clenched his fists and stood straight up, pushing the debris away as fast as possible.

Dustin lifted his arms and instead of flames and bullets, the weapons shot forth streams of liquid nitrogen. The knights had no defense against the mixture of heat and the sudden introduction of the horrid cold that now came down on them.

The fires around them went out as the first shots of nitrogen exploded into a gas, but the continuing stream of the chemical turned their armor into something resembling glass. The high pressure of the streams shattered them on contact as he did his best to not get Sparky caught in the attack.

Once he was clear of enemies, at least for now, he turned off his weapons and looked around, realizing he turned this whole place into an icebox and one stray shell could bring it all on top of him. He knew it was time to leave. Carefully, he made his way out of the building. Sparky realized this and followed Dustin outside as well.

"Chill out," he said, looking at his new frozen sculpture, impressed with himself.

## 43

Across the battlefield, a soldier was looking through binoculars and saw Dustin emerge from the other side of a building that had been frozen with white steam coming from it, and his eyes widened.

"Sir, you need to see this. I spotted the Orange target. It's got to be the same one that attacked the train station earlier," he said to Captain Will, who was in the middle of trying to regroup his forces from the surprise attack.

He stopped what he was doing, looked through his own binoculars, saw the same thing, and narrowed his eyes.

"Damn it, you're right, paint it. Call in the air support to take that one and all the machines surrounding it down. Kill them all," Will said but didn't stop looking at the enemy.

"Yes, sir," the soldier said and got on the radio. "This is Omega Company requesting fire, 600 meters to the west of us. We have a laser painted on the target," the soldier said into the radio.

"Fire incoming in thirty seconds, stand by," a voice replied.

"You'll pay for what you did," Will said and watched, waiting for the firepower to come down and wipe them all out, and he couldn't wait for it. Until now, he was reluctant to call in any kind of help due to how bad the situation was, but this was worth it.

Dustin didn't realize he was being watched or was in any kind of danger when Sparky, with no warning, latched onto his right arm and took flight. Dustin was about to protest, but then his armor detected the incoming attack too late to do him any good.

Everything was obliterated in the area in a terrible blast that followed. Only a field of fire remained.

Dustin was saved by Sparky's quick actions, but the two of them didn't get far as the shockwaves knocked them both out of the sky and sent them into the ground, where they became buried in wreckage seconds after they hit.

"Thanks, Sparky," he said with a groan. Everything hurt. Dustin decided that getting up was a bad idea and knew that attack didn't come from any machine. The military was out for his blood, not that he could blame them.

"Well, great. I knew that distraction thing would come back to bite me later. Now there are two threats to deal with. This is not my day. You'd think they'd let stuff go already. It was so many hours ago," he said, frustrated with the annoying tenacity the army had.

Dustin didn't see any kind of power source come up on his scan. Nothing but the energy signatures of machines detected in the area, and it was frustrating, like everything else today.

Something else was catching his attention. From the eastern sky, the blazing light of the sun was beginning to be seen through the small cracks of his temporary tomb. The light was filtering through the clouds and the smoke to make all the surroundings appear bright red.

"Time is starting to run out. I better get a move on," he said and tried yet another scan, but still no sign of any power source anywhere in the area.

"Are you kidding me right now?" It wasn't anywhere near him, according to the scan of the area. He was at a loss as to what to do.

"Oh, why didn't I think of it sooner? I'm an idiot." He sat up, pushed the debris off him, and looked towards the ocean, and there it all came together. It was under the water.

"Of course. The fire guy gets the water mission because that makes perfect sense," Dustin said in frustration and looked at the cat.

"Sorry, you are going to have to sit this one out. Thanks for saving me back there. Listen, if I make it back out of the water, find me. If I don't, you should find a nice, quiet place to live and stay hidden because the world is a mean place, and I don't want you ending up in some lab somewhere," Dustin said. Sparky understood, then ran off.

Dustin turned back to face the water for a second, forgetting that he was almost wiped out by a massive attack and was still being watched. "Screw it," he said.

He took off running as fast as he could and hoped for the best. The battle was resuming as the machines provided their counterattack. Their blue eye beams burned through the red sky. No one paid attention.

Running with the armor made for a fast trip. About midway through the run, he noticed that he wasn't making a loud clanging metal sound as he went. It was all about the small things in life, he supposed.

Before he knew it, Dustin was at the water's edge. Behind him was the rising light of the sun. For now, no one cared about him. It was something that wouldn't last long, he figured.

"I sure hope to hell my armor is waterproof," he said and took a deep breath. Summoning up the courage to face whatever was under the water.

He walked into the ocean and watched on his internal screen as the status was updating as he waded into the dark. His armor, thankfully, was sealing itself. "They think of everything," he said with a small sigh of relief as his head disappeared under the waves.

As soon as he did, he had the overwhelming urge to shut his eyes to keep the water out. Inside the armor, all he could see around him was black, and he could feel the dull cold through the metal armor. It didn't take long for his eyes to adjust as he walked deeper into the ocean. He could hear something long before he could see it.

The sound alone made him want to run in the other direction. It sounded like something was constantly moving in the distance—big, metallic, grinding against itself somehow.

It made his skin crawl and reminded him just how much he hated the ocean and how full of weird things it was. Dustin walked until he came to the edge of a cliff, and it was there. A massive, black, multi-armed machine based on sea life but resembling none he could remember.

It was something horrible, and he couldn't help but wonder how long it had been down here and no one noticed it. The power source and his target were in the center of the thing, and below it was a great red orb that looked like a giant eye.

The enormous tentacles were discharging bolts of power in the water that were powering all of the busy machines who had unknowable tasks. These were more fish-men than actual people. He took a deep breath, steeling his nerves.

"Ok, squid, thing, whatever. Let's rock."

Dustin decided to try and get this done as fast as he could, even if he had no idea how he was going to do it. He pushed himself off the ledge and started to swim towards the monster.

Dustin could see as he got closer that each tentacle was eighty feet long and now could tell that there were five of them connected to the orb body. As he swam closer, the machine's gigantic red eye turned in his direction.

The tentacles began the process of opening hundreds of

compartments at the same time, and each one was home to its own personal laser cannon.

"Oh crap." Was all Dustin had time to say as he noticed them opening before they all fired at the same time. The black ocean filled with the bright blue light of hundreds of laser beams. He dropped through the water, spinning around, trying to avoid being torn to pieces.

"Damn, not going according to plan, not like I had a plan to begin with. I hope my future self is better at planning."

He pointed his wrists at the enemy to try and return fire, but nothing happened.

"Damn it, are you kidding me right now? I need options, armor. Give me something I can use." A blue laser grazed his left arm, cutting a tiny piece out of it as he twisted. One hole in the armor underwater and all the healing factor in the world wouldn't save him from drowning.

He knew that there was no way to make it to the surface from these depths as fast as he needed to, not by normal swimming anyway.

Dustin was going through the list as fast as he could. It wasn't until he got to the search and rescue mode that he found something that might be useful. Cutting lasers.

He figured if lasers worked for the enemy down here, boiling the water as they went, the same would work for him. He selected the option and was amazed that instead of the wrists, his visual monitor activated a targeting system, and he realized that these cutting lasers were eye beams. The bright orange beams burned through the water and struck the nearest tentacle, but to his surprise, the laser beams reached the black skin of the thing and did nothing.

Dustin fired again, but nothing happened. "Stupid useless laser cutters," he said and continued his descent into the abyss with no idea what to do next. His only form of attack was useless. There was no way he could get close with the constant barrage of enemy laser fire coming at him as he sank.

Dustin hit the bottom and discovered that the machine stopped shooting at him. He could see its black outline with his armor's help, otherwise, it would have been invisible. It was now that he noticed his energy levels, for the first time, were falling.

"Weapons don't work, energy recharging is down. I don't know what to do," he said and looked around for something that might be useful but didn't see anything, not even fish.

"Never any random useful things kicking around the bottom of the ocean when you need them," he said and looked back up. Then he got a terrible idea.

"Looks like it's the only thing I can do, and this. Oh, this is going to suck. Armor, set the nanites to make sodium, as pure as you can get it," Dustin said and clenched his fists, put his arms down at his side and fired. There was no point in counting to three.

The chemical reaction was violent, the explosions sent him in the direction he aimed for, and this was all he could do. Turning himself into a missile was the last thing on his tactical option list in his head, but it was the only thing left he could think of to do. Life was overrated anyhow, he supposed.

The underwater explosions were anything but stealthy. The squid bot saw his approach at rapid speed and prepared to attack again. Dustin had no room to maneuver at this ever-increasing speed and hated that this would boil down to dumb luck.

It fired on him and was trying to track his movements, but his increasing speed made this impossible. Dustin flew over it and never got to see the results of his actions due to how fast he was going.

The laser cannons fired at Dustin and missed. The cannon fire shredded the monster's body in several places.

It was about now that Dustin stopped firing the pure sodium into the water and turned around to see what he did in time to see the massive thing give off one last, great blue death ray into the ocean floor, then explode with a blinding white light.

Dustin was thrown through the water as the explosion sent out the shockwaves, and he slammed into the ocean bottom, headfirst, to be buried under the ground. "Not a good day." He pushed himself up through the mud, hoping that he got the job done.

All he could see were enormous chunks of the monster falling amongst the black cloud of what he hoped was oil and not some kind of exotic mutating chemical ooze.

The last thing he wanted to see was mutant turtles or worse showing up in the future, maybe mutant sharks. He shuddered at the idea.

"See, no trouble at all. I got this down like. Oh." Dustin was cut off when he noticed that the power source was still glowing, and now all the rest of the machines were closing in on him. He was sure that they wanted revenge, and there was no escaping them. That little stunt drained his energy. He wouldn't be doing something like that again any time soon.

"Does it ever end?"

Now he had to make a mad dash to the power source. It was a race he knew he had no chance of winning. One of the swimming things dived at Dustin, and he got a better look at it. They were greenish-gray and appeared to be a mix between a fish and a person. Knowing what he knew, he could only imagine that there was some miserable soul trapped under that metal like all the rest.

The thing reached out with its clawed hand. It was clear it wanted to rip Dustin's face to shreds. He grabbed the metal arm with his right hand, spun around using his left arm to push the thing into the ground by the back of its neck, and in the same motion applied pressure to snap the neck. He felt the thing go lifeless in his grip and dropped it.

"I have a power source to catch," he said and realized that he talked to himself more than he should and wondered if anyone was listening on the other end. He hoped not, but it wouldn't matter much if he ended up dying down here.

Refocusing, he pushed himself off the bottom to swim towards his target as fast as he could.

"You know, metal heads, I am getting sick and tired of this," he said as three more came from above. He reactivated his cutting lasers and fired in a wide arc after targeting them. To his surprise, they didn't even attempt to get out of the way as the lasers sliced through them all with ease.

He didn't know why they all didn't attack at once, it didn't make sense. It was as if some kind of control was broken when the big squid went down, and the humanity was breaking through on some of them.

It was the only theory he had to work with, and maybe those who were attacking thought it was better to die than to keep living like this.

Some were chasing him, and he in turn was chasing the machines trying to escape with the power source. That was his mission. How it lived through the explosion, he didn't know. They had unlimited energy. Dustin was running low. Cut off from the air and the ambient energy that came with it, it was obvious that the armor was not meant for long periods of time underwater. He needed to put an end to this.

All he had to do was get above the surface to recharge, but if he did that, he could lose too much time and fail the mission, dooming the world at the same time. It was too big of a risk.

Dustin cleared his mind and focused on the chase. Too many random things were running through his head, insane ideas. The ocean always inspired a special kind of terror in the squad, but none of them could quite understand why. Its secrets were best kept hidden from them and everyone else.

It wasn't long before his armor began to tell him that to go any further would result in instant death due to being crushed like a bug from the pressure. He was hoping that the machines had similar limitations of their own, and instead of heeding the pressure limit warning, he tried to swim faster. Dustin almost smiled when the two let the blue cylinder go and turned to face him, but then he realized they wanted a fight.

"I don't have time or the air for this," he said and backed off a bit. The two lunged at him through the water. He shot up as they advanced and spun around to grab the one closest. He put his arms around its neck and twisted until he heard the strange sound of crunching metal and bone underneath.

Human or not, they shared the same weaknesses. He let the metal body go and disappear into the black. It was a distraction, and Dustin looked up in time to see a metal fist run into his head and send him end over end in the water.

The metal gill man didn't bother grabbing onto him, and it gave him time to recover. He couldn't help but think it was the person inside that saved him.

Dustin shook his head. Oh, what he wouldn't give right now to be on land because this would be so much less complicated. The fish hybrid charged at him again, and Dustin sighed and steadied himself.

It swiped its razor claws at him, and Dustin twisted out of the way, grabbed the offensive left arm, squeezed it, and attempted to throw the thing over his shoulder but put so much force into it that he tore the limb off, creating a cloud of black inky fluid. He spun around and slammed that limb into the side of the head of his enemy, knocking it into the distance. Dustin was sure this battle was over and dropped the makeshift weapon without hesitation.

The power source was floating away from him when he turned around and looked at it. "You're not going anywhere."

He swam deeper to get the capsule. The pressure was intense, and every movement felt as if he was swimming in liquid steel.

His armor was at its limit, and he could feel it weakening. Dustin reached out with all the strength he had left and grabbed onto the capsule with his left hand, to what looked like a handle.

"Alright, need air, dry land. Let's get you out of here," Dustin said and started to kick in the opposite direction toward the surface. Then he thought he was going insane. He was hearing voices and couldn't figure out where it was coming from until he looked back down toward the power source. "What the hell is up with this?"

## 44

It wasn't long before Dustin dragged himself back onto the shoreline and dragged the blue capsule behind him. The second he was on the shore, he dropped to his knees, then to his side, and let the capsule go. He and his armor were out of energy, and all he could do was wait until the recharging system kicked back in.

"Let me out of here, damn it," someone on the inside yelled again. At least it sounded like that.

"Oh, shut up in there, you'll be fine," Dustin replied and looked at the still glowing capsule. He couldn't do anything, even if he wanted to. He needed to wait a few seconds before the power began to flow into his armor. He slid his helmet back to take a deep breath of smoke tainted air.

"Nothing like the smell of California smoke and war in the morning, that's for sure," he said as he willed himself to sit up, no matter how much he didn't want to.

Whoever it was inside was still pleading to get out and was going into some kind of shock-induced panic. "Shut up in there, they'll hear you. Hell, I'm tired of listening, Christ," Dustin said as he slid the faceplate into place.

He pointed his right wrist at the container, shot his zip line through the top of the container, and pulled it back and to the side to tear it off. The clear fluid spilled out, and the kid came with it. A teenage boy no older than fifteen, he was sure of it, soaked in the boring clothes they took him in. "Oh, thanks for letting me out. What the hell took you so long?" he said, coughing between the words, then turned around and saw Dustin standing there.

"You're just another machine." He tried to scramble away on his hands and knees, but Dustin grabbed him by the back of the neck with the armor's superhuman speed. "No, you're coming with me," Dustin said and spun him around to see all the lifeless metal ships on the ocean.

"You can come with me, or you can take your chances with them. They want you for something, and until I know what it is, we can't let you get caught," Dustin said, and the kid looked back at him, getting the point. "Fine, let's—wait, what do you mean until—" the kid stopped in his tracks and jumped back as a knight was moving down the beach.

"We need to run," he said, and Dustin crossed his arms with a shrug. "It's just one. Stand back, I got this," he replied, also having some rage built up.

"Just one? It's seven feet tall. It's bigger than you," he replied. Dustin ignored him and stepped forward. "Alright, you virus that learned how to walk. It's time to do something," Dustin was so frustrated that he couldn't think of something witty enough to finish that sentence with. "Syndicate tech detected. Objective, destroy all Syndicate tech," it said in a jagged, inhuman voice.

"Yeah, tell someone who cares, because I don't," Dustin said and winced at his own words a little. He lifted both of his wrists. The knight ran at him at full speed.

"Orange dude, you better move," the kid said, and his jaw dropped when Dustin fired twin streams of liquid nitrogen at his enemy and watched it freeze in place. Before it fell over, Dustin leaped forward and smashed his fist into the knight's chest, shattering it into pieces all over the sand. "Yeah, that's more like it, something, like I said before," Dustin said and turned back to the kid.

"See, one, not a big deal. Now let's get out of here," he said. There was no way he was going to let the machines get him back. Dustin thought about killing him too, but he had no idea if the metal infection could reanimate dead things. Keeping him alive was the best choice for now.

"Dude, you are so awesome. Do you have a code name? Can I have a code name? I want to be called Vector. No, Vortex. No, well, something that starts with a V because that's the coolest letter of all time, and that's what I want. What's your code name? Do you have one? You saved me, and I don't even know your name."

The kid was so excited to be saved, and to be saved by such an awesome looking suit of armor, he went from panicked to obsessed fan in seconds.

Dustin's left eye twitched.

"My code name is Flame Genesis. Now, what the hell were you doing in that tube thing?" he asked. "That is the best code name ever," the kid replied with the same amount of enthusiasm. Dustin nodded and motioned him to get on with his side of the story.

"I don't understand it, but here is all I remember. This weird looking robot guy broke into my house a few days ago and told me I was chosen by something called the 'Delta Force,'" he said and looked down. "He, it, whatever it was, killed everyone. I remember now," he said, wincing as the memories came back.

"I don't understand it any more than I do now. He said I was special and that he needed me for a mission. Everyone was dead. There wasn't anything I could do," he said and looked around at the smoke filled sky, still in shock.

"The machine took me, and I met four others. One by one, we were put into these tube things," he said and looked at the broken capsule again.

"The next thing I know, all hell is breaking loose when I wake up, and here we are," he said and tried to smile.

"We'll be friends forever now, right? I mean, you saved me. You must be a superhero to do that."

The kid was still trying to be excited about meeting an actual real life superhero of all things and thought he was special.

Dustin almost wanted to give this kid the 'I'm not a hero' speech, but he didn't after hearing how he saw his family slaughtered. Maybe he could be nicer.

"Alright. We need to get you some place safe. Well, safer than here at least," he said, then heard the sound of metal and turned around in time to see Sparky standing there, his claws extended, ready to tear the kid to shreds.

"Whoa, don't kill him yet. If he talks too much, bite him or something," Dustin said, hoping that Sparky wouldn't go insane and eat him. The kid and the cat gazed at one another, one with terror in his eyes, the other with cold and murderous intentions, even for a machine. Dustin didn't know if it was jealousy or something else, but now wasn't the time for this.

"Hey, you two, we need to get out of here, and it's a long walk out of enemy infested territory, if 'out' even exists anymore," Dustin said and thought about bringing him to the military, but he would tell the exact same story.

This story was not something anyone else needed to hear, and if someone was choosing potential future Delta squad members, the enemy knew far more than they should have. He wanted to call Cody to report this update, but there was no telling who was listening in. He was always paranoid about things like that when he was sober.

For now, it was best to keep quiet about it. Dustin didn't know where safe was, but he wanted to find it sooner than later. He picked the kid up and put him on Sparky's back. "Not going to carry you anywhere, but it's faster than walking. Let's go," he said.

"This is the coolest," the kid replied as the three of them made their way off the beach.

## 45

Cody's target was deep in the city, and he had no idea what it could have been. His armor had been putting him on a wild chase. The target appeared to vanish when he thought he was getting close.

This time had been no different as he peered over a roof to see nothing. "Of course."

He realized what time it was. The sun was coming up.

Cody dropped to the street level and backed off into the shadow of a building to make his next plan. Attention was the one thing he didn't need What he needed was time to think. All this running around was pissing him off.

"Stupid tech, stupid armor." Cody was relying on it too much. He let it all go to his head. It was time to go back to basics. He retracted the armor. The blue goop disappeared under his skin. It felt itchy for a second. "Weird." Cody did his best not to think about it.

With the armor gone, he stepped back into the morning light and walked down the sidewalk like it was a normal day. If he couldn't find trouble, he'd wait for trouble to find him.

For a few minutes, there was nothing. Even the sounds of distant battle decided to take a break. Maybe the war was already lost, and he was behind the times. He wished someone would keep him updated. He was about to contact the others when the silence was broken by heavy footsteps. Cody got close to the wall and looked around the corner.

Six knights were walking away from him, but he didn't want to take the chance they had some kind of scanner. He almost didn't follow them until he realized they weren't moving to the outside of the city. They were going back. They had to be going somewhere. There was always the chance they were malfunctioning, too.

That'd be the case, knowing his luck. Still, the chance had to be taken.

Cody waited for the metal soldiers to turn in the opposite direction before he crossed the street. Following a bunch of machines was easier than expected, if not boring. Cody was seconds away from blasting all of them when they made one more turn. He stopped in his tracks. "What the hell?"

It was the La Brea Tar Pits.

The knights he was following took their place in a wall of living iron. They formed part of a barrier and stood like statues facing all directions surrounding the building, protecting it with a square perimeter, and there was no telling how many there were.

Cody reactivated his armor, slid his hand down to his weapon, and had no idea what to do next, but he knew there were only two options: try to find a way past them all or blast his way in.

Even if he got in, he knew that getting out would be next to impossible.

"Alright, I guess if you need to walk into Hell, you might as well kick in the front door." Cody took a deep breath, started walking towards the enemy fortress with his weapon at his side, and almost felt like someone right out of an old western movie.

"Hey." The outer ring of knights turned their heads in his direction.

"Yeah, I'm talking to you, steel for brains," he said loud enough to get anyone's attention, and it worked. The machines kept staring but wouldn't leave their posts yet, and he knew it.

He lifted his plasma cannon and fired into the line of knights and watched as his beam hit a shield and deflected in all directions.

"Really?" Cody was disappointed at how that turned out. He was expecting more destruction.

"So, you're the future, I guess? The perfect race hiding behind a shield against one lone and amazing commander of super soldiers? I understand if you're afraid," Cody said and stopped walking. "I'd be scared too if I was up against me," he said to the metal men behind the shield and waited. It didn't work. They didn't budge.

Cody didn't know what else to try. "What is this shield made out of, and can I break it?" he asked his armor and waited.

"Frequency eighteen on the plasma cannon will penetrate the ion shield, but there is no safe way to get you through the shield until you find the generator. The generator is located inside the main complex," his armor said, and he sighed.

"Great."

He pointed his weapon at the enemy again. The armor set his weapon to the right frequency, and as soon as it was ready, he fired. The bright blue beam sliced through the shield and drove into a metal body, cutting in half lengthwise.

"Bit of a strange angle on that one," Cody said as the attack made them realize that defense wasn't an option anymore. Cody counted seventeen of them in all as they started to run at him. It was easier to kill them if they were running at him, he supposed.

He knew that he had to stand his ground. "Today is full of bad ideas," Cody said as the first three machines crossed the shield line. At that same time, he fired to watch the mechanical knights dodge. "When did you get so athletic?"

Two of them jumped to the side, but the one in the middle jumped at him, over the plasma beam. Cody looked up in time to see the metal fist slam into his face. It knocked him to the ground.

"You're the commander of what, super soldiers, really? You're useless without this second-rate armor," the machine said in a clear, deep voice. "My armor isn't second-rate, you take that back," Cody replied as the enemy put its foot into his chest.

"Yes, it is. Worse, it's blue. I mean, blue. Who dressed you for school, your mother?" it asked and increased the pressure on his chest. "Nope, this was all part of the plan," Cody replied, but he had no plan.

## 46

It was about to talk again when Cody realized that he still had his weapon in his right hand and managed to lift it up between the legs and fired.

"See, planning, don't leave home without it," he said, stood up, and pushed the melted remains off of him in time for white eyebeams to hit his chest. The impact knocked him twenty feet straight back.

He hit the ground hard, cracking the cement as he did. The pain wasn't so bad, but those beams did something to the nanite makeup of his armor.

Everything went black on the inside, and his vision flickered back on and off, each time revealing the ever closing image of a giant walking towards him. Seeing them or not, he could always hear them.

Cody didn't realize it but without power, his nanite armor was heavy. He couldn't move an inch. "Well. I admit it. I should have taken this approach differently. I don't know if you can hear me, but I could use some help. Anytime now would be good. I hate to be a pain, but I am calling any nearby Delta members. Commander down, I guess," Cody said, and all his dreams of being the big shot hero taking on an enemy stronghold all on his own went up in smoke.

He was sure this was their big, save-the-world mission. The Cyranthis thing was a warmup. This mission was their destiny, their legendary event in history. Never once did Cody imagine he would be taken out in one shot.

He underestimated his enemy and his own power. It was a dangerous mistake anyone could have made, and all he could wonder as he waited for death was what he was thinking and, more importantly, why.

Cody supposed it didn't matter anymore. His armor was stuck in a constant cycle of rebooting, and in a few seconds, he was going to have his brain smashed into the ground.

His head was stuck turned to the left. He could see in glimpses the machine approaching him and was sure that this was the end. The thing stopped and stood over him.

In between the glimpses, one second the knight had a head, the next it was falling to its knees as the head exploded into a black gooey mess. "God damn."

Cody did his best to look over. He saw Blake in the distance, pointing at his sniper rifle and shaking his head in disappointment as the dead metal fell on top of him. Cody hardly felt the impact or the weight of the enemy. He could only smile, thankful, as someone showed up.

He didn't expect any help at all in this situation from anyone but didn't know why that thought ran through his head so often. Now he could focus on his glitch prone armor for a second and try and find out what was wrong with it.

## 47

Wyatt ran from the other side and from behind. He hit the enemy in the back, sending blue and black ooze. The thing fell to its knees.

"What, you were crying like a bitch, we had to wait until the last minute to save you. You know, the big damn hero moment they like to do in movies or books, for example," Wyatt said, pulling out the blade and laughing after he proceeded to remove the knight's head with another clean cut.

"But when we're done with this, we need to talk about your planning skills. They need work," Wyatt said and knelt down to the armor to see if he could figure out what was wrong with it as he pushed the remains off of the commander.

"Dustin, if you're around, you need to get over here. Commander went stupid and needs some help. He broke his armor," Wyatt said into the com.

"Yeah, I'm here. I need to take care of something, be there in a second," Dustin replied, and Wyatt had a good idea what that something was.

"Fine, Blake and I will run defense until you get here. The rest of them are coming to join the party," Wyatt said and stood up to face the enemy.

"Guys, listen. Their beams are what did this to me. Don't let them hit you," Cody said but had no idea if they could hear him or not, but he had to try anyway. "Don't worry about it, bro, even I'm smarter than you are. Not getting hit is on the top of my what not to do list. Seems you need to check your priorities, Cody," Josh said, and Cody rolled his eyes.

"Yeah, like I knew that the enemy could shut me down. I'm not psychic, jerk," Cody replied and wasn't appreciating the verbal assault he was being forced to take.

Dustin knelt down next to the commander. "Oh, yep, it looks like you've been hit by something bad here. You're magnetic. The nanites are fused. I can fix this," Dustin said and stood up, not saying how. Cody was getting nervous but couldn't move an inch.

"It's going to get a little hot in there, so just hold on a second. Maybe hold your breath, too," he said and pointed his wrists at Cody. He let loose twin torrents of fire. Cody flinched as the heat increased inside his powerless armor.

"Dude, what the hell are you doing out there?" Cody asked as he felt as if he was going to burn to death in this armor. "Heat kills magnetism. Shut up and take it like a man already," Dustin replied, keeping the fire going.

Despite the insanity of the situation, his armor did its reboot cycle and this time it worked like it was supposed to. "It's working. Stop the fire at any time."

"I like burning you with actual fire since I'm not good enough to do it with words," Dustin replied, laughed, and killed the fire at the same time.

Cody sat up, his armor still smoking from the flames. He looked around to see the others in battle all around him, but with this shield, there would be no point to any of this even if they won. Cody needed to make up for this failure he made earlier and stood up. The battle was fierce, the enemy was distracted.

There was no way he could have asked for a better situation

than this. "What's the plan?" Dustin asked. "That base has a shield. My beam can cut through the shield. I think there's one plan. Thanks for getting me back in the fight, but now I need to finish what I started," Cody replied.

Dustin shrugged. "That did nothing to answer the question. You're worse than a politician at a debate," Dustin replied.

Cody ignored him, put his finger on the trigger, and took off running in the direction of the shield wall. He wasn't quite sure where it started, so he fired his cannon in front of him and cut a hole through the energy wall.

He ran as fast as he could and jumped through the hole his cannon made and landed face-first into the cement. Not wasting any time, he broke his way into the visitor's center and saw the shield generator there, maybe.

It was a strange-looking cylinder-shaped device about four feet high that had three prongs on it, each tip glowing orange. It looked like a generator anyway. He had no idea what a shield generator was supposed to look like.

Cody walked up to it. The strange humming sound it made felt important. He clenched his right fist and put it through the weak metal in the middle. Sparks flew from the hole he made for a few seconds before it powered down.

The shield flashed blue for a second before it fell. "Thank you."

# 48

Cody walked outside to check on the battle. It was over. He was going to explain some things, but before he could take another step, he heard a click. It was the kind of click that made his heart sink because it was a familiar sound.

"God damn it." From behind, there was an explosion, and it took him off his feet, flinging him into a tar pit.

"Everyone is our enemy today. I don't know about you guys, but I am getting sick of all of this. We should go back to that stupid tower and end this already," Dustin said.

"You think? Wow, I never would have thought that up on my own. You're a regular genius," Josh replied. Wyatt was going to say something, but he was interrupted by a sloppy sound. "What the hell is that noise?" he asked. The others heard it too and decided to check it out.

Walking around a corner, the four of them could see Cody doing his best to claw his way out of the pit. They laughed.

"Oh, shut the hell up," Cody said, pulling himself out of the mess. "Just not your mission, is it Commander?" Josh asked. Cody flung excess tar at him. "What the hell, now I'm all sticky too, you jackass," Josh said. Cody crossed his arms.

"So, did anyone get the power source McGuffin thing?" Wyatt asked, doing his best to change the subject. He looked around and it was hard to miss all the mechanized reinforcements that were surrounding them, and took a step back.

"No, I didn't get it," Cody said, "I only got the shield generator."

Dustin looked at both of them. "This just isn't going to do. I need to clean you two up a bit," he said, pointing his wrist at both of them and without any warning let loose a jet of orange flame in their direction.

"Dustin, wait!" Wyatt said too late. Josh and Cody's armor caught fire and the trails they left behind caught on fire as well. The tar pits caught fire. Everything around them was turning into a slice of hell on earth. Burning mammoths and all.

Josh's armor wasn't as covered as Cody's was. Cody was covered in uncontrolled fire and fell to his knees. The heat was far more intense than Dustin anticipated. Cody was in no shape to be dealing with this. The nanites in his armor weren't fused. The flames passed through them in a thousand different places. Cody flailed around in pain for a few seconds before falling to the ground.

"What the hell were you thinking?" Wyatt asked.

"I just wanted to get the tar off them. I figured fire would do the trick," Dustin replied as he smothered the flames with thick white mist. He hoped that Cody wasn't too fried underneath that worthless blue armor of his.

He supposed they were all experimental. Maybe the commander had some bad luck. There was so much he didn't understand right now.

Wyatt wanted to beat Dustin within an inch of his life, but the horde didn't care about any of their drama.

"Dustin, Josh, you two provide cover for our retreat. Blake, take out the power source, and I'll get Cody out of here. I'm faster than all of you. This is an order. Go," Wyatt said.

Nobody liked the idea of retreating from a fight, but due to Dustin's inability to think about stuff before he did it, they had no choice.

"Fine," Josh replied and took a breath. The two of them went to face the metal horde.

"Dustin, shoot me again, I will break your neck. I don't know if we can heal from that, but I'd rather not find out, got me?" Josh asked as he walked, the flames dying on his blood-red armor. "You could try. Besides, I'm sure we can take a broken neck or two," Dustin replied, and Josh ignored him this time.

The heavy metal footsteps approaching them were a bigger concern than Dustin was right now. It was no fun being trapped between fire and metal, and he hoped that Wyatt had an escape route planned because he didn't know where they were going from here.

"You ready?" Josh asked.

"As ever."

The horde created a target rich environment. The two of them scanned the area for a second, then began to shoot at any who managed to break through the wall of black smoke.

Even for them, this was proving difficult. Without their armor, it would have been impossible to see anything through all of this. They both knew their bullets were useless against the machines, but there was more than enough force between their weapons to knock them down.

The roar of their miniguns tore through the air as if it were coming from a massive angry beast thrashing about in anger. The bullets hitting the metal sounded like a heavy rain on a tin roof.

"Guys, work faster. Dustin lit a huge signal fire, and I think every damn robot in town is coming in our direction," Josh said as he knocked a half formed machine off its feet. "I'm working on it, don't freak out. You know as well as I do these power sources can't be smashed open," Blake replied.

"Yeah, get it done. We need to go," Josh yelled, trying to be heard over the guns.

Dustin almost felt bad about being so thoughtless. The only thing he could do about it now was defend the others, but he knew it wouldn't make up for his mistake. On the other hand, he still wasn't sure this was real. It could have been one of those no win simulations. It felt real, but Syndicate tech was impressive.

## 49

Blake approached the capsule and he punched. His fist stopped against the glass and it actually hurt. The electric pulse fired off and knocked him into the far wall and he hit the floor.

"All right," he said, and got back to his feet. "The hard way."

He unlatched his rifle, fired at the far edge of the thing, but the bullet deflected and hit the wall, leaving him confused.

"What, are you kidding me right now? What's the deal with this one?" He needed to figure out something else and fast, so he did the only thing he could think of. He jumped to the top of the capsule where the metal covering was and looked for something that resembled a hatch or lever, but it was all smooth and black up here, all useless.

There was no electricity up here, so Blake tried his first plan again. He knelt down and started to smash his left fist into the metal.

It began to give way at last. Blake hit the surface. Three times he smashed the metal. On the third time, the glass below gave way to the pressure and shattered.

He watched the kid fall out of it and he jumped down into the slime. The sound of gunfire was getting closer now.

"Guys, I'm going to get to the drop off point, meet you there," he said and picked up the boy with one arm and walked to the wall where he was slammed into. He kicked straight through it, leaving a hole. He walked through the hole as the smoke poured around him, turned on his cloak and it cloaked his passenger as well. Would it do any good? He could only hope.

"Let's go, kid." The two of them left the battlefield together.

Wyatt grabbed the commander's arm, lifted him up. The second they made contact he could see all the vitals. Cody was a mess on the inside but alive.

Wyatt didn't want to move him, but he had no choice in the matter. "Come on, now for my next trick, we need to get out of here. It could prove difficult."

He listened to the ambient sound of war. There was a pattern to the shooting, waited for an opening. It wasn't a long wait.

"Here we go, commander."

He threw Cody back towards the building and he sailed through the air to land on the hard ground. Through the broken glass doors and next to the broken shield generator.

"What, you thought I was going to carry you on my back? No. You're not worth that much to me," Wyatt said and wasn't in the mood to play heroic lifesaver today.

Cody groaned in terrible pain.

"Did you just throw me?" he asked in between coughs. Wyatt jumped the distance and soon landed next to him. "Yes, I did. I just tossed the commander. Don't worry, I'll be sure to tell them that you took a rocket to the face or something. You'll never live this day down, if we live through it," he said with a laugh and helped him stand up.

Cody wasn't eager to stand but he did so anyway after a few seconds. "Diab and Emo, we are moving out. Let's go finish this madness once and for all," Wyatt said to the others through the intercom.

"Did that shrimp just call me Emo?" Josh asked and

twitched. He had it with his teammates. The stupid plans, the listening to the bad guys, all the running around. This should have been done hours ago. All of this was stupid, all of this was pointless, and anyone had the nerve to insult him, here, now? Screw that.

He stopped shooting at the enemy and pointed his weapons in Wyatt's general direction. Then he began shooting at him and the commander. "Nobody calls me Emo. Nobody, you ninja wannabe," Josh screamed inside his armor.

Wyatt acted fast and picked up a fallen knight that was nearby and the bullets slammed into it and changed into shrapnel as they were made to, but the shield was effective, for now.

"Josh, buddy, use your words. I don't appreciate this. It's ruining my day. At least shoot Dustin instead, we both know this is all his fault," Wyatt said and couldn't believe that Josh was having his emotional breakdown now of all times.

"Never call me Emo again. Or I'll kill you," Josh said and turned to look at Dustin, who in turn could feel those icy cold eyes on him and he hated it. He knew that he was going to get shot at any time.

Dustin didn't want to be shot, he did the only thing he could think of, tried to remind him of reality.

"Josh, you can shoot me later, but we need to leave, now," Dustin said and he snapped out of the rage. "Fine, let's go."

The two of them took off running from the battle, having bought enough time. The machines weren't far behind, but slower and far less agile.

## 50

"God damn it," Wyatt said leaning against a wall. "What's the matter with you?" Dustin asked and Wyatt wanted to punch him.

"Shut up," Wyatt replied.

"Guys, I'm tired of playing babysitter, are you coming or not?" Blake said through the intercom. "Yeah, yeah, we're almost there. Wyatt needs to catch his breath," Cody said. Truth was, he did too.

"Fine, hurry up," Blake said and cut the communication. Somewhere nearby a tank fired, something exploded. "This whole city is going to be burned to the ground," Dustin said.

"Doubt it, there's a lot more city than you think. I can't say much about downtown," Wyatt replied.

"We cool?" Wyatt asked. Josh looked at him. "Yeah, you're right. It's all Matchstick's fault anyway," Josh replied and stared at him.

"Sorry, sometimes I do things without thinking," Dustin replied. "I think that's true for all of us," Cody added.

"Come on, let's get out of here before this turns into a romance novel," Wyatt said and pushed himself off the wall. Cody could feel his burnt skin start to peel off under his armor.

He was glad he didn't have to see it, but at least he was feeling better.

They used their ziplines to make it to the rooftops. In every direction all they could see was rising smoke and burning buildings. It looked as if Los Angeles was close to being ready to take its rightful spot in Hell.

"What a wonderful scene," Dustin said. No one could tell if he was being sarcastic or not. There was panic in the streets, they could hear muffled screaming in the distance too.

They knew that anyone found trying to leave the quarantine zone would have been shot on sight. There was no telling how many people were going to be killed by American bullets today. The number was high, and more importantly, forever classified.

It was clear there was no safe place in Los Angeles today once the sun revealed the full scope of the invasion. "I hate this," Cody said.

"It'll all be over soon, one way or another," Wyatt replied.

With the sightseeing out of the way, they moved to the west, away from the bulk of the destruction and madness consuming the city.

They got to an apartment building, abandoned when they found it earlier, still abandoned now at least for all they knew it was, anyway. It wasn't like they checked all the rooms.

Vector, or Vortex, he hadn't decided yet, was staring out the window to the streets below. He held a metal bat in his hands, ready to beat down anyone who dared come inside. He was even willing to take on a machine if he had to. The others were keeping to themselves, still too scared to talk about much.

The front door opened behind him and he didn't ask any questions. He attacked. Cody came through the door and got hit in the face with the bat. The metal bat dented on impact.

"What the hell," Cody said and grabbed the kid by the neck and picked him up with his left arm with ease.

"Whoa there killer, it's us," Dustin said, and Cody looked at him as the others walked into the apartment.

"What, wait, what is going on? Why are we here anyway? I just thought you had a place to regroup," Cody said. He set his would be attacker back down. "The others are in shock, but fine as far as I can tell," Blake said.

Before anyone could say anything else, Vortex spoke up.

"Well, you see. Me and them, we have something called the Delta Spark, and the robot came to get us. The bastard killed my whole family in front of me. It didn't look anything like the ones Flame Genesis and I saw on the way here. He looked different. Oh, I'm Vortex. Or Vector, I haven't decided yet," Vortex said, and Cody glanced at Dustin, who in turn shrugged.

"Well kid, how come you're awake and these ones are, uh, catatonic?" Cody asked him. His reply was the same as Dustin's, a shrug of the shoulders.

"These five have potential?" Blake asked, looking at them.

"Yeah, apparently the Delta Spark thing can be detected. That's how those two on the tower must have tracked these ones down and used it for their power sources," Dustin said, but he was guessing the only thing that made sense.

"Those are some sick twisted bastards. What happened to that one?" Josh asked as he pointed to the one with the burn and Wyatt sighed.

"When I got him out of that cage thing, my aim was too good, and I got him in the shoulder. I had to fix him with fire or risk bleeding to death," Cody shook his head at this news but wasn't surprised.

"I sure am glad you're not the medic. So, these five could be our replacements?"

He didn't like the idea of being replaced, especially with machine infested people.

Vector, on the other hand, could hardly contain his excitement but kept his mouth shut the whole time. "We can leave them here and when they wake up, we'll let fate deal with them. Whatever will happen, will," Blake suggested then, sure they would recover from this if they had delta potential at all.

"We can't be this squad forever. Eventually, someone is going to replace us. The jumpy one standing over there, he's going to be the new Hell Razor, I can tell," Wyatt said and laughed a bit.

"That one talks a lot and was obsessed with the letter V. Just like Wyatt," Dustin said and looked at Vector, or Vortex, or whoever.

"Hey, I'm not obsessed with... Oh, right," Wyatt went quiet.

"Well, we have a job to do. The sun will be going down in a few hours, and I think we can do this thing ahead of schedule," Cody said. He was still in serious amounts of pain, but he played it off like he was alright.

"Vapor, you need to make sure nothing happens to them until they wake up, okay?" Cody said, and the kid was happy about this.

"No problem!" He started looking for a new weapon when Wyatt pulled out one of his throwing knives and handed it to him.

"Use this but be careful with it. Machines are tough, and you'll only get one shot," Wyatt said. The kid took it. "Thanks," he said, and with that, the five of them left the room, having no more time to waste.

"Are you insane?" Dustin asked over the intercom so Vapor couldn't hear.

"Don't worry about it. They'll be fine. This will all be over soon," Wyatt replied, "besides, everyone has to grow up at some point," he finished.

"Good luck, kid," Cody said, breaking up the conversation and leading them back out the door. "Give 'em hell!" Vortex yelled back as the door closed behind Blake.

## 51

They shot their zip lines to the building across the street and began moving in the direction of the tower. "We'll put an end to this," Wyatt said, and Cody nodded. "Yeah, but I need to take care of something. I need to, uh, shed some of this burnt skin. It's driving me nuts," Cody replied.

"TMI, bro," Josh replied. The others groaned.

"Just hurry up," Wyatt said, and they took off.

Cody nodded and waited until they were out of sight, then he turned around to look at the apartment they had left.

"Nope, can't trust them. For all I know, they're infected by the machines," he said, pointed his weapon at the building, and shot at the bottom. It caught fire.

Cody knew that by the time they realized anything was wrong, it'd be too late. There'd be no escape. He watched as the fire grew. "It won't take long."

He fired his zip line and moved off the building to catch up with the others. They didn't get that far away.

"Alright, guys, let's finish this," Cody said as he landed on the roof behind them. Wyatt wasn't stupid. He looked back where they came from and saw the smoke. Wyatt glared at him.

"You guys keep going. I need to talk to Cody here a minute, alone," Wyatt said.

"Fine, don't take too long. You know how Dustin gets when he has to stop and think for a few minutes. He shoots everyone," Blake said as he fired another zip line, and the others followed him.

Wyatt drew his blade and put it to Cody's throat. The commander didn't move. "What did you do?"

"I did what was required, the job we all have. Those kids were tainted. Could you imagine a tainted squad, filled with revenge?" Cody said and kept his calm as Wyatt pressed the sword against his neck.

"No, I know you don't want to imagine that nightmare." Wyatt didn't know if he should kill him or not.

"You committed murder to prevent what could be. What gave you the right?" Wyatt was furious.

"Leaders make hard choices. It's why you're not standing on the end of this blade. It's why you'll never have to take more responsibility. It's why you're second in command because we both know you don't, nor have you ever had what it takes to make choices like this. You can go back and try to save them if you want, but remember the true threat is waiting on that tower. We are almost home. Do you want to put it all at risk for people who could be a problem later?" Cody asked, and the two of them stood there in silence for a few seconds before Wyatt put his blade down.

"After this, I'm done. You may be fine with it, but I'm out, and I am sure as messed up as the others are, they'll be with me too," Wyatt said and put his sword away.

"We'll see how it turns out," Cody replied. "You know if you would have killed the potential threats when you found them, we wouldn't be here now," Cody said.

"Shut up," Wyatt replied and took off running to meet up with the others. Cody shook his head and followed him. The others were only two rooftops away.

"What was all that about?" Dustin asked.

"We were discussing who was going to buy the beer when this mission was over, that's all," Wyatt replied. Dustin laughed. "Man, you know I got that covered, don't even worry about it. Let's focus on more important things," he replied.

"I'm with him," Josh said.

"Does anyone ever seem to notice how time seems to move faster when you're trying to get somewhere in a hurry?" Dustin asked as he looked up at the sun.

"Yeah, what's your point? Less talking and more moving," Blake replied.

## 52

It wasn't long before they stood at the place this all started, in front of the Bank Tower. The streets were torn up from the battle. There were plenty of bloodstains left behind, but no bodies, machine or human. This fact alone was unsettling, but they had to focus on the task at hand instead of what might have happened here.

"They'll see us coming, you know," Wyatt said.

"I bet they left hours ago," Josh replied. "Sent us on a damn fetch quest like idiots, and they ran off," he finished.

"Nah, they are expecting us. They wouldn't run, right? Let's go say hello," Blake said, and instead of trying to go the stealthy route like they did last time, Cody started walking towards the front door.

"Are you sure the front door is a good choice? Isn't that kind of like walking into a deathtrap and—" Dustin was cut off as Cody turned to look at him.

"No," he said and turned back to the tower entrance. He walked up to what remained of the doors and tore them off the hinges, throwing them to the side.

"Let's go," Cody said and walked inside. "Into the deathtrap we go," Dustin said.

The tower was empty.

The enemies remained true to their word and didn't try any traps to keep the squad busy. Cody was almost impressed, but the trip up was taking forever, and he was beginning to regret taking the stairs. It was easier in power armor. You could jump up and skip entire flights at once.

The seventy five story trip took about ten minutes. When they didn't have to avoid any machines, it was much faster. They reached the roof of the tower once again to find it empty.

"Well, now what? We did all that running around and there's nobody home?" Wyatt said and looked around.

"Maybe they got scared once they figured all of their bases belonged to us and ran. I hate it when they run," Dustin said, but as soon as he said it, they heard footsteps from behind.

"Yeah, typical luck," Dustin said and turned around with the others.

"Look who it is. The Syndicate dogs always do what they are told even if someone else tells them to do it. You are stupid, but annoyingly successful," Dawn said as they approached.

"They do it too well. Better than we thought they would. Maybe we should tell them that the whole power source thing was a joke? Those kids didn't have enough delta potential to power a light bulb for longer than a week. Those machines would have burned them out anyways and the real power source would have begun to work in a few hours here," the metal man said and laughed.

The whole squad was stunned, but Cody had a horrid feeling rise up in him. "No," Wyatt said and couldn't help but look at Cody who in turn could do nothing but look at the ground.

"The leader and the sword boy know what this means. I can see it in their helmets. It's too bad the other three have no idea," Dead Steel said and crossed his arms, his metal face was frozen, but his words sounded like a smile.

Josh looked at Wyatt and Cody, feeling as if he was missing something important.

"Oh look. It's ten minutes to midnight," Dawn said and looked at the sky. It turned from black to a dark green as the energy began to build up.

"Everything is going according to plan, all that's left is to kill you five and finish the job," Dead Steel said as the bright green thunderbolts leaped across the sky in wild formations without a single cloud in the sky.

"Now the power of metal will be felt throughout the whole world. Today is the day the world that is, dies," the metal man screamed up into the sky with a sense of overwhelming victory. Dawn took a step away from him in embarrassment. He didn't notice.

"Yeah, someone's world ends today, but that doesn't mean it's going to be ours," Blake said, having had enough with all the talking and boasting. He pulled his weapon and fired at the lady. The bullet never reached her. It melted into a silver puddle and fell on the roof.

"Oh, did you forget that I have power over all metal? In a world dominated by steel, I am the new Goddess that you'll all worship," Dawn reminded them, but something didn't make sense. Their armor was made from metal. Cody caught the brief look of confusion on her face.

"Guys, she can't kill us how she wants. We can take these two down and end this before it gets any worse," Cody said, hoping he was right about this, and the five of them pointed their weapons, reasserting their original intention.

"Commander, how are we going to kill them if we can't shoot them?" Dustin asked.

"Dustin. Stop being an idiot," Cody said. Dustin was then reminded that bullets weren't the only path he could take.

Dawn was trying to collapse their armors in on them, but she couldn't assert her will over the metal of the armor, and she was beginning to wonder what it was made out of.

A vibration assaulted the tower, only for a second.

"They must be here already, coming to complete the plan. It's time," Dawn said and smiled. Wyatt didn't like how Dawn said that and walked over to the edge of the roof and looked down.

"Well, hello there, mister invincible. Thanks for not destroying my body. Now I can use it to kill you," Sprocket said and was running up the side of the building. It leapt over Wyatt and landed behind him.

Wyatt turned around to face him and was disappointed. He hoped he'd never have to see the minotaur again. "Alright, fine. Have it your way, not sure how you lived, but I can fix that," Wyatt said. "Dude, a minotaur, that's awesome," Dustin said, and Wyatt winced. "Yeah, this one likes to kick," he replied but didn't take his eyes off it.

From the other side, the machine leader in his red cloak came over the edge. "It appears they have made me a liar, and a killer too. This doesn't sit well with me," David said, and looked around at the situation, not knowing why he was reactivated, but he didn't care.

"You should get out of here. We can take it from here. We don't need to do this," Josh said, hoping this time things would go better. At least he wasn't thirteen feet tall yet.

"No, like I said before. I fight for an entire race, like you. Our battle must go on, but as before you against me," David said and prepared himself. "Damn it, if that's the way you want it, fine." Josh knew what this meant and got ready to fight again even if he didn't want to.

"Something is wrong, where is the ocean--" Dustin cut Dead Steel off. "Oh, you mean the squid thing. It wasn't as smart as you'd hoped. It committed suicide when it tried to kill me. Unlike the rest of my squad, I know how to finish a job," he said while taking his weapons out.

"Now it's you and us and those two I guess," Dustin said as Blake and Cody looked around. "Were we not worthy enough to get something special to fight against or what?" Cody asked.

"About that, you two were the least threatening of the group, a sniper and a washed up commander? I might as well say it, I know who you are, Mark. The rest of your squad is going down. While I was in the lab, I saw these armors in development and knew who they were for. I could control metal, don't you think I would have learned a few of your secrets along the way? I'm getting my revenge on the Syndicate, and there's no better place to start than with breaking its favorite toys," she said.

Cody was shocked at this news and almost wanted to correct her, but she didn't need to know Mark had gone insane, and they were the new group.

The lack of current information was an advantage Cody wasn't about to give up anytime soon. Although he wasn't sure how it was an advantage.

If they broke the code and revealed their identity, would all of this come to an end? He doubted it. Crazy didn't have any instant fixes.

"Well, if you see the commander and the sniper as the weakest parts of the group, your plan was doomed to fail from the beginning. The Delta Squad doesn't have any weaknesses," Cody said and pulled out his plasma cannon, pointing it at her.

"It doesn't matter, I'll kill all of you myself if it comes down to it," she said, and he could feel her insanity, or maybe it was anger growing by the second.

## 53

Wyatt and the minotaur faced off, and he was well aware that he almost lost last time. "Goodbye, Sprocket." Wyatt readied his sword, and the minotaur clenched his iron fists.

The two ran at one another at full speed, but the machine fell to its side and slid across the roof, leaving a trail of dark blue behind it.

There was a gaping hole in its side that was gushing the blue blood. Wyatt looked over to see Blake still aiming at the beast, nodding at Wyatt.

"You can thank me later, stop playing around and let's get to work," Blake said, and Wyatt would remember to do that. He walked to the bleeding, if you could call it blood, Minotaur. "Enjoy the climb back up," he said and kicked the thing over the side. Then he turned his attention back towards the real threat.

Josh and the leader were already in combat, but this time it was different. Neither of them could fly, and it was a long way down to the ground.

"Come on, man. Just let me shoot that thing and get it over with," Blake said. "No, you wouldn't understand. This is a fight to the finish between two honorable opponents, something somebody like you wouldn't know much about. Now come over here and help us end this," Wyatt replied.

Blake turned his attention. Now it would be four on two, odds he didn't mind. Blake didn't care much about honor or fair play.

He didn't have time to deal with the mental issues of his team.

Dawn was laughing at the whole thing as a bright green bolt of energy flashed behind her. "You dare challenge the new ruler of the planet so soon. Are you that eager to die?" she asked in a sweet and sinister voice. It was so full of arrogance that it made Cody cringe.

"Well, I suppose we do. I mean, we don't have anything better to do right now," Cody said and looked to the others, and they all shrugged a bit and kind of mumbled an agreement.

"You'll take us so lightly, it won't happen again," Dead Steel said. The machine was showing his humanity more than ever now.

"I liked this plan a lot better when we had them outnumbered. Maybe we should retreat and start over?" he asked her. She looked at him.

"Oh yeah? That is a good idea. I think we should run away and-" she smashed her fist into her partner's face and sent him sailing into the air fifty feet before he started to fall, disappearing into the dark green sky.

"Zeron always was cowardly when it came to the endgame. I used them to get to this point. I was never interested in genocide anyways. The machines would suit my purposes for this. Observe humans," she raised her hands to the sky. The team looked around the city. From all points, there were thousands of liquid silver lines coming from the city.

"Come to me. Come to me and let's show the whole world who the new ruler is," she screamed into the sky, clearly lost her mind.

"Do we shoot her now or wait until the weeb trash anime move is done?" Wyatt said. Cody shrugged.

"I guess we can wait, she worked so hard to get here. It'd be a shame to ruin it at the end, right? We need to be sensitive to our enemy's feelings. I read that in a book somewhere. I think it was *How to be Woke*. I still don't know what woke means," Dustin replied.

"You're an idiot, Dustin," Blake replied.

## 54

Josh and the red leader didn't notice any of this going on. They were in combat when it happened. The leader's arm began to melt away into nothing, and it was spreading. Josh watched his enemy melt away into nothing and took a step back.

"Looks like this is the end. It was an honor fighting you," David said as Josh looked at him and shook his head. "This isn't fair, what's going on?" He was confused at what he was seeing. "Life isn't fair, but make sure yours goes on after this night, alright?" With those final words, the once honorable machine was nothing but a stream of liquid silver metal. Josh picked up the red cloak without saying a word, then turned his gaze.

"You."

He pointed at her and dropped the cloak as he got his weapons ready to fight. If there was a point when rage turned into hate, this was it. He began his march towards the last remaining enemy.

"Oh man, look what you did. He went into his rage again. Why'd you have to go and do that? Not bright of you to do that. We could all die," Dustin said and was worried as he watched, knowing full well Josh had plenty of reason to kill him. Josh needed little reason to kill anyone if the mood was right.

All of the strands of steel came down as if it were rain. It came from every direction and was surreal to see liquid metal like that flying through the air, almost maddening. Reality wasn't supposed to be like this. This mission and the last one made them wonder if reality itself wasn't beginning to break down.

Dustin was afraid they might have broken the world.

Sometimes the bright green lightning would hit the metal and travel down it into her form that was being covered with steel, sending green arcs of power around her and into the roof of the building.

"Hey, I don't think you should just walk up to her and--" Dustin tried to convince Josh not to do what was coming next, but it was too late. Without even thinking about it, Josh lifted his arms and opened fire into the metal form only to watch the bullets melt and join her growing form.

"You have failed," she said as her left arm melted into a long silver tendril and slammed down as Josh sidestepped out of the way to the right. Dawn took the advantage and formed her right arm into a similar tendril, swinging it in a wide arc. Josh was getting his balance when he was struck in the stomach.

The force of the impact knocked him off the side of the building and into the darkness as if he were little more than a child's toy.

"One down, four to go. How about that? You guys are turning out to be worthless." She focused her attention back on them. The others were impressed and shocked at the same time that something like this could even happen.

"Well, now we know what not to do. Let's take her down nice and fast," Wyatt said and charged. Nobody else was thinking the same way, so he was the only one who charged forward into battle.

"Uh, maybe you shouldn't do that. We need a plan," Blake tried to tell him, but it was too late. "Cody, you want to do something here? A plan would be nice, you know, something," Dustin said, and Cody shrugged.

"I want to see how this goes first. It'll be fun to watch Wyatt get his ass kicked, don't you think?" he replied. "Maybe, but not like this," Dustin replied, never taking his eyes off what was happening. Dustin did have a plan, but his team had some issues to work out, so he'd wait his turn if he ever got one.

Wyatt's sword slammed into her metallic chest and stopped on impact, doing nothing. "Aww, look at that, you want to play with me. Didn't your mom ever tell you to buy dinner first?" Her left arm reformed into a hand and grabbed the blade, pushing it down and away. At the same time, she sent her steel knee into his stomach.

Wyatt felt this attack through his thin armor and doubled over on impact. A second later, he found himself being thrown into the opposite far side of the roof where her partner went over the edge. He stopped himself by digging his sharp-edged armor into the roof before going over, too.

Armor or not, he was sure that a fall from up here would kill him. He was thankful for the zipline.

The rain exploded from the sky as Wyatt stood up. The water was infested by the green energy as it fell, sparking out long before it hit the ground. It appeared that every star was falling at once in a shade of bright but fading green fireworks display.

"Any suggestions, Commander? Or do we keep doing this the hard way?" Dustin said. Cody crossed his arms. He was lost in thought about something else. Whatever it was, Dustin was frustrated by the lack of a response.

Dustin decided to act when Cody wouldn't, even if it was only a split second of silence that had gone by. "Alright, I have an idea. Attack, all at once!"

The others looked at Dustin as if he were insane.

"Who died and made you the commander?" Blake asked. He was still worried about Josh's fate more than the battle.

"Trust me, I have a plan." This phrase was more than enough to make all of them worried about their immediate future.

"Alright, I don't know what this plan is, but we'll do it. Delta Squad," Cody paused and couldn't believe what he was going to say next. "Attack, you know. All at the same time, probably something we should have tried first," Cody said, following Dustin's lead but wasn't sure why.

## 55

Three of them ran at the silver queen. Their bullets weren't going to work, so they had to get physical. Dustin waited for his chance. A metal spike tore through the roof of the building and shot through Wyatt's right arm. The blood went all over the soaked roof.

The sound of his blade hitting the ground was heard through the falling rain. Another slashing sound could be heard when a different spike from the same source tore through Blake's right knee and out the back. There was a muffled scream under that helmet.

Again, the blood poured on the roof, and the sniper fell. Dustin prepared to make his move when from over the edge of the building, Sparky flew over the side with Josh holding on to its back.

"Sparky, you, hey, how are you still alive after the metal maniac did her thing?" Dustin asked, and was distracted. Sparky tilted its head and blinked at him.

"What is this thing and what's going on?" Josh asked.

"That is my friend. His name is Sparky. I don't know what's going on myself, but if you excuse me, I have to go save our friends," Dustin said and focused on the task at hand.

"You, saving someone? What happened? Did the world end or are you and I the last two members left?" Josh asked in disbelief but was ready to change his tactic after being taken out of the fight with one shot earlier.

"Oh shut up and pay attention. You might learn something in the rage addled brain of yours," Dustin replied. At the same time, a bright blue plasma flash took place and cut a large gash into her body.

Dawn recoiled in pain as her metal covered body was shredded. The wound closed up, leaving no blood or any actual sign of physical damage. "Do you think that anything you do to me can hurt me? I am invincible. I am a goddess and immortal."

She looked less human every second and more like an abomination from beyond reality as the metal still continued to pour in from around the city and attach itself to her body, increasing her mass. A long steel tendril wrapped around Cody's neck and lifted him off the ground.

Dustin knew he needed to wait longer. The time wasn't right yet.

"Josh, I know this is not what you want to hear, but my plan can't work yet. She needs to be more pissed off and draw in all the metal even faster. She needs a reason to collect the metal faster, you need to help them."

Josh didn't want to go over to the now multi tentacled steel demon, nowhere near it, especially at Dustin's command. On the other hand, Dustin was confident in his plan, and it was the only game in town right now.

"Fine, but you owe me," Josh said and jumped off Sparky, charging the silver and black monstrosity. Josh jumped into the mass of steel, channeled all of his strength into his right fist, and punched Dawn in what appeared to be her face, at least he hoped it was.

Her metal mouth opened, and it was filled with long, razor-sharp teeth on impact and closed around his right arm as another head formed above the one that kept Josh in place.

This attack made the spikes retract from the other two at once, and Cody was dropped to the ground with a thud.

"You dare strike me? You should have stayed dead," Dawn roared at him. Two tendrils erupted from her sides, turned into solid spikes, and impaled him through the stomach, tearing through his armor and coming out the other side.

Blood came gushing out of both ends and poured onto the ground as she lifted him up into the air, letting his mangled right arm go in the process. There was too much blood and too much pain. He tried to pull the spikes out of him, but it was useless. He couldn't even tell Dustin to do whatever it was he had planned.

## 56

Dustin saw what he was waiting for. The metal had finally stopped flowing.

"Alright, rusty. It's time for you to go. You've had your fun, and now it's got to stop. Just looking at you gives me the creeps," he said as he walked forward in her direction.

"Rusty, me? Look at you. You are the color of the stuff and--" he cut her off.

"Bitch, it was an expression." Despite the rain, he lifted his wrists and fired.

The second the liquid nitrogen hit metal, twisted, vaguely female body, it began to freeze solid. This didn't cause any pain to her, but it did make her black and empty eyes grow wide and, in a panic, she threw Josh to the side. She lunged at him with countless silver tentacles with incredible speed, but Dustin wouldn't back down.

He was relentless with his attack, and that icy stream from his weapons did their work long before they could reach him.

The others watched this and realized what his plan was, but it was hard to see what was going on. The nitrogen was freezing everything it touched, and in rain like this, it was looking more like an actual winter instead of a typical California one.

In seconds, the horrid metal monster was nothing more than an ice-coated statue. Josh was in serious pain, but his healing factor had already kicked in, and he struggled to stand. Dustin shut down his weapons in time to watch Josh run forward and smash his mangled right arm into the massive bloated and frozen steel form with whatever power he had left.

The whole thing shattered. The steel fell to the ground in frozen chunks, leaving behind an unconscious woman on the roof in the snow, as she appeared before all of this happened. She was still breathing.

The others limped their way towards her.

"She is too dangerous to be kept alive," Wyatt said as he picked up his blade and prepared to kill her while he had the chance.

"Yeah, maybe. We only have ourselves to blame for this. The people we work for did this," Blake replied, not sure what to do.

"Do we kill her or not? I mean, she'll wake up and want to kill us again. I'm sure this plan won't work twice," Dustin said. He didn't want to see this all be for nothing.

"Yeah, we should be better than our enemies and let her live," Cody said, but wasn't sure how to do this. How did you restrain someone like this?

With no contact from Blackfire Island, he wasn't sure how to proceed from here.

Wyatt looked over at him, and the grip on his sword tightened. "Better than who exactly? You killed those kids, you set the building on fire, how are we supposed to be better than machines?" Wyatt asked, and this drew an uneasy silence among them as Wyatt came out with what he knew.

The idea of killing innocents over what turned out to be nothing and letting a monster live, victim or not, to him was unforgivable, and he decided the others should know too.

"You didn't do that, did you? He's lying, right? You didn't kill those kids?" Josh asked and was in complete shock at this news.

Cody looked away.

"Would you want any potential replacements being driven by revenge? The greatest team to ever walk the planet be bloodthirsty from the beginning, tainted by machines? No. We would all feel responsible for that, and who knows how many people would have been killed because of that? I did the right thing. I don't care what any of you think. I am the commander. It was my choice to make, and I made it," Cody said.

The other four backed away.

"So what, you would kill us too if for some reason the Syndicate screwed us over and we wanted some payback?" Josh asked and aimed his remaining weapon at him.

"You're kidding me, right? We want to do this here, now? Metal chick over there could wake up at any time and you want to talk about maybes?" There was no response from the others. They were more than upset at the commander for doing such a terrible thing.

"Dustin killed soldiers, remember? Shot them all up for no reason. Where's the outrage for that?" Cody asked.

"I didn't have a choice. You know the code. No witnesses, we don't exist," Dustin replied. Sure, he knew there were better ways to go about it, but he didn't want to think about it right now. He could hardly believe Cody would kill a bunch of kids. "And I did?" Cody asked.

"They were kids, no one would have believed them anyway," Dustin replied. It was clear there was only one way to work this out.

Maybe this was a simulation. Maybe it was time to change the code.

## 57

Cody's armor opened up, and he stepped out of it covered in his own blood and ashes from all of the damage he took over the course of the day.

"Well, if you have something to say, let your fists do the talking. Words never did much good. This is the only language you understand. If you have something to say, now's the time."

They looked at one another. "Fine," Wyatt said. He'd wanted to do this ever since he saw what Cody did. One by one, they stepped out of their suits. The air burned their lungs, the chemical smell, the smoke, and the unnatural cold.

The machines that had served them this whole time were put to rest. "It looks like we'll need replacements after all," Wyatt said, knowing that things could never be the same.

None of the Squad remained untouched in the course of events. Their wounds were healing, but they were covered in their own blood in various places. They had been awake for too long, and they were all exhausted, fueled with a new kind of rage towards their commander. What he did, they would make him pay for it.

"You know, maybe he was right after all. I don't feel right fighting against the commander. We don't need to work together anymore, but I don't think we should do this," Josh said. Even if Cody did a terrible thing, they were still brothers. He was doing his best to contain the rage here. It wasn't easy.

"True, you can feel free to sit this one out if you want," Dustin replied, not looking at him.

Josh wouldn't sit this one out. He would take a few steps and stand beside his brother. "Three on two, we still got you two beat," Blake said.

Cody ran in Wyatt's direction and sent his left fist towards his head, but Wyatt was too fast. Speed was his strength, but not thinking ahead was his weakness, too.

The commander knew Wyatt well enough. The second Wyatt blocked Cody's fist, Cody spun around and sent his foot into Wyatt's stomach, and he doubled over. Cody used his right fist in the form of an effective uppercut that crashed into Wyatt's face, sending him into the air, along with the blood.

The whole event took a few seconds. "Stay down," Cody said.

Blake and Dustin barely had time to register that Cody had even attacked. Once they did, it was decided that Josh had to go down first. It wasn't personal, it was that he was defending the wrong choice. The two of them rushed him at the same time.

Josh grit his teeth. It had been a long couple of days, and he was tired of fighting, tired of everything. He hoped they were too.

Dustin was slower. Josh bolted past him and attacked Blake instead. His right fist blasted into Blake's face, and they both fell to the ground.

Josh was on top, intending to smash Blake's face in. He clenched his right fist, and his left was around Blake's neck, trying to choke the life out of him. Josh looked into his eyes and knew this wasn't right. Deeper than knowing it, he could feel how wrong this would be, and he hesitated for a second.

Dustin wasted no time and put his hands together. "Get off

him, you mongoloid," he yelled the first thing that came to mind.

He swung his combined fists into the side of Josh's head and knocked him down into the thawing surface with all the power he could muster. Josh slid away, but not far.

Blake was still choking from the attack and could only see Josh's outline rising in the rain through his blurred vision. "Damn it," Blake managed to cough the words out as he struggled to stand up. Laying here, he might not get so lucky again, but he knew that if Josh was hesitant before, there was no chance of being that now.

Dustin's blindside attack would have only pissed him off even more.

Josh's slow walk burst into a run. Dustin didn't have much time to think about it. The hulking rage beast of a man snarled at him. "Oh," Dustin said. The blow to his head must have shut off the human side of his brain.

With nowhere to retreat, Dustin did the sane thing and ran forward. Dustin punched Josh in the side of the head. It drew blood and made his head turn to the right, but he grunted and spit out the blood. The look in Josh's eyes wasn't human anymore. Dustin could see violence in them.

Josh lunged forward with a vicious, slow haymaker. Dustin ducked and punched him in the stomach. It was flesh, he thought, but under that shirt, it still felt like iron. "Damn," Dustin said as Josh grabbed him by the back of the neck with one hand. He spun, never letting go. Then he thrust Dustin's face into the roof of the building, smashing his head into the surface covered in jagged ice. Each blow was worse than the last. The roof of the tower was beginning to crack.

Josh was expressing himself with inhuman rage with each blow. Something primordial was below the surface.

Blake could see Dustin getting his head smashed in through the rain.

He also realized the sky was still green and whatever was

about to happen was still going on. They might not have accomplished anything. "Damn it, guys," Blake muttered to himself. He knew that there were more important things going on here than their issues. He had to find a way to bring it to an end.

Wyatt and Cody didn't notice the sky around them or what was going on with the others. Wyatt threw a punch. Cody weaved out of the way, wrapped around his arm, and bent the limb in such a way that it broke. The sound of the snapping bone was barely heard over the scream. Cody pushed Wyatt back and to the ground.

The fire in his arm was intense, but Wyatt wasn't bothered. He'd felt it before and worse. He straightened his arm. With a sick crack, it snapped back into place. He held it as the healing process began and stood up.

"Give up yet?" Cody asked between breaths. "Never," Wyatt replied and took off running forward in the rain, drew back his left fist, and swung, broken arm and all. Cody moved forward and blocked it, realizing too late this was part of Wyatt's plan, and the other fist swung even faster.

Cody looked away when he was punched in the face and stumbled to the right before falling over.

He looked into the rain and saw in the distance a man in black with glowing blue eyes standing there unaffected by the wind or the rain. His entire face lit up in a great green flash of lightning, and he had a horrible sinister smile that sent chills down his spine. The man in black gave Cody a thumbs up. At least it looked like that from here.

With the next bright green flash, the man was gone. Maybe this was all in his head. It's been a long mission, and he was tired.

"Who in the hell was that?" Cody asked himself as the whole world around them started ending. Everything started to shake.

## 58

An earthquake was occurring. It was enough to get the Delta Squad to stop trying to kill one another and stand up despite the strange quake. It lasted a few seconds, then it was still again. Done almost as soon as it began.

"Did anyone see that?" Cody said and looked at them, but they were all looking at him. No one was interested in any more of his delusions.

"Are we done now?" Blake asked, and no one was willing to reply at first.

"Yeah, one last thing to take care of, but we're finished after this," Cody said, and no one was willing to disagree.

"Right, so I'll be leaving then," Dustin said in mumbled words. His face had been brutalized, and even though it was healing, it was hard to look at.

Josh stared into the bloody mess and then down to his hands. He was going to say something, but Dustin turned around before he could, blood mixing with the rain as it hit the ground.

"Damn, you messed him up," Blake said, and Josh wiped his own blood from his face. "He'll be fine," Josh replied, then started walking back to his armor.

Wyatt and Cody glared at one another. Wyatt was feeling a

great sense of disappointment in Cody. All he wanted to do right now was cut him into pieces, but it wouldn't have done any good.

The sky around them still had a sick green glow to it, but no one cared. Blake even looked around but couldn't stand to be around these people anymore. Not after this.

He and the others walked towards their armor and sealed themselves inside.

Wyatt was the first to turn and jump off the tower, only to remember that his arm had been chomped on earlier and his zip line function was broken.

"Damn it." He had to figure out a better way to land before gravity did it for him.

Dustin decided he was done. His face was still torn up, everything hurt.

"Come on, Sparky, let's get out of here. I need to find you a nice place to live. It's the least I can do," he said. The metal cat was curled up, close to the edge. Even if it was a machine, it looked scared. He couldn't blame it.

Dustin jumped off the roof as well, and the metal cat followed him off the edge.

Blake looked at Cody.

"You have issues. You should get your priorities straight. That metal bender down there would have killed us all. I'd shoot her now, but because of your last stupid order, I'll follow it. I don't know why, but I have a feeling all of this will come back to bite us. You have a good life, turn yourself in," Blake said before turning invisible.

Cody was going to say something, but he watched as the outline in the rain faded away.

"No jail can hold her, and the Syndicate can't be allowed to have her back. I'll take her away from here. You deal with whatever is making the sky green," Josh said, then walked over to Dawn's body and picked her up. "I am so going to regret this."

"Yeah, I'll take care of it. Oh, don't tell Mom and Dad, okay?" Cody said.

Josh turned to look at him but didn't say anything. Then he ran off into the dark.

Commander was alone. He thought everything had made sense at the time, now nothing did. They all left him, and he still didn't understand why.

He was doing his job, that was all.

## 59

Cody stood alone in stunned silence when something began to crackle in his helmet. Someone was trying to get through.

"Cody, come in. This is Heath. What is going on?" Cody heard it but didn't understand why communications would be coming through now.

"Cody, come in, answer me," Heath demanded again, and it woke Cody up. "Yeah, I'm here," Cody said and looked around.

"Listen, something is happening above me. It's making the sky green and discharging massive amounts of power. The threat down here is over, but can we do something about this?" Cody asked.

"Satellites say it's static electricity. Congratulations on your victory, but where are the others?" Heath asked him, and Cody didn't know.

"You'd know better than I would at this point."

The sky above him lit up in a blinding white flash. Cody didn't bother looking. When it faded away, the sky was less green now, and the rain was the only sound he could hear this far up.

"Heath, the squad, this version of the squad is finished. Start looking for a new one."

There was silence for a time. "What do you mean finished? We're reviewing the data now. Everything is lagged. Tell us what happened."

"Bad things, I did my job, followed the code. I'm leaving my armor on the top of Bank Tower. Send a drone to pick it up or something. Once you get to the end, you can come look for me, or not." Cody's armor melted off of him and formed into a small blue capsule in his left hand.

"You weren't that effective anyway. Maybe the next version will be better for someone," he said and tossed it. It landed next to the last melting piece of ice on the tower. Cody turned and walked toward the exit, destination unknown.

Dustin ditched his armor after activating the homing beacon so the Syndicate could find it in the hollowed out shell of an office building. "Hopefully, they find it before the Army does," he said. The suit didn't look good anymore, used and tired. Thankfully, Sparky didn't tear his throat out the second he was alone and revealed to be a person instead of a machine. The thought was always in the back of his mind.

Dustin hopped on the cat's back, and together they flew out of the city. Even at this rapid pace, the two of them still had to avoid helicopters and any spotters on the ground. The rain did its job and concealed them both. Dustin smiled. The cold rain on his face felt great, and for the first time in a long time, he felt free.

The pair of them made it out of the city and landed far from the action, and for the first time, Dustin had a chance to look at Sparky for more than a few seconds without any distractions.

For the life of him, he couldn't figure his mechanical friend out. It was still unlike any machine he had ever seen, at least before tonight.

Most notably, on its shoulders, a large Z was on top of a six-pointed star. It wasn't the mark of Zeron, but that was all he knew.

"Whoever built you might come looking, but for now, you need to stay somewhere no one will bother you. I have the place," Dustin said and patted Sparky on the head. Despite being made of metal, he was warm to the touch. Dustin picked up a stick and carved some coordinates into the muddy gravel road.

"Can you get here?"

Sparky shot a red scanning beam over the numbers, then wiped it away with a metal paw. The two of them stared for a few seconds. Dustin smiled, and after a few seconds, the metal cat turned around and disappeared into the trees.

"Good luck."

Dustin turned and walked down the road. He had no idea where he was going to go now or what he was going to do. He wished he had a coat right about now, in any case.

Josh took Dawn to a broken place in the city. She had woken up after leaving the tower. It wasn't too tough. Both of them looked like they were victims, covered in blood, dirt, and burn marks. They blended in.

"So, I am giving you a once in a lifetime chance to live quietly," Josh said as they walked down a broken street. "I have no reason to take your offer because--" Josh cut her off and revealed a large, sharp piece of wood in his hand and brought it to her throat.

"Or I can kill you right here. You were running, remember? They can catch you if they realize you had anything to do with this. You need to stay dead and gone—no attention, no powers. Disappear."

Dawn realized two things: one, he was right, and two, this was not the squad she was looking for. She wasn't sure, but something told her that this was true. The ones she heard so many stories about—well, she wouldn't be standing here if this were part of the team she was looking for.

"Fine, I'll stay dead." She turned to look at all the destruction she had helped cause, and it wasn't even for the reason she had intended it for. "Good, I'll hold you to it." Josh said.

"About the whole war on Cyranthism, the thing that everyone forgot about in this whole mess, what did you mean by it?" Josh asked. She looked to the sky.

"I don't trust it or any religion. My idiot partner thought it'd get your attention faster. As if a machine knight falling into the city wouldn't be enough," she replied. "If we wanted to, it would have been so easy to take over the world. All we needed to do was lay low, infect people all over the world. By then, it would have been too late for anyone to stop," she finished.

"It never was about taking over the world. That kind of tech could have solved a lot of problems, but now it'll be buried in some Syndicate lab, never to be seen again if we're lucky," Josh replied.

"Yeah, what a waste," she said with a shallow laugh. "What are you going to do now?" she asked. When she turned around, he was gone. "Oh."

With a soft sigh, she walked down the street alone, looking for the first crowd to blend in with and disappear.

# EPILOGUE

President August got the news hours ago. The threat was over. Even now he didn't understand the whole story. The chances were good he never would, but that was fine with him. The story he did get would have to be enough. He read the speech again, not sure who wrote it. Even the paper felt expensive.

The crew behind the camera started the countdown, and he took a breath as the silent part started. Then the little red light on the camera came on.

"My fellow Americans. The biological attack in Los Angeles is over. America is safe again due to the heroic efforts of the men and women of the military and first responders. Martial law will be over in the coming days, and the rebuilding of Los Angeles will begin," he said, trying to look as honest as possible.

"Those who were responsible for this terrorism have been killed, and they will never again threaten us or anyone else. Before you celebrate, please remember all those who have lost their lives in the worst terrorist attack in American history, and the worst in the history of the modern world." He had no idea if that was true or not. It was what the paper said.

"I'd like you to keep California in your prayers tonight. More information will be coming soon. Until then, stay safe, and good night," he said, as the light switched off.

The president's short and to-the-point speech didn't win anyone over, but it was the news the world was waiting for.

"Great job, Sir," someone said, and he smiled. "Thanks," he replied despite not doing much at all.

Thousands of people would be reported missing and would never be seen again in the city of Los Angeles. Rumors of monster machines circulated throughout the country, and videos even came up on the internet. The Syndicate and the government crushed all visual evidence that showed up online as they monitored it often.

The official story was that a deadly nerve gas was causing mass death and intense hallucinations, making people believe they were seeing everything from machine people to strange lights in the sky.

Of course, rumors always persist, and the truth would never completely die out, especially on the Deep Web.

The president's speech was coming to an end on television.

A man sat there in a dark apartment with his left hand on an ancient book, fingers tapping the cover.

He shut the television off. His golden eyes gave off their own light. Someone had lit the fuse, they almost succeeded too. It was almost time.

The phone next to him rang, and he picked it up. He listened and smiled at what he heard.

"So, they broke up the band, and you think you can keep the program derailed? This keeps getting better. Thanks for the update. I'll need some willing volunteers to get started, but you can leave that and the rest up to me." The man with the golden eyes hung up the phone.

"Well, book, I hope you are as advertised because we have work to do," he said, opened the book, and began to read.

# ABOUT THE AUTHOR

I wrote my first "novel" when I was 16 years old in High school, it started out as something I just wanted to try, but the thing ended up saving me in English class when I told the teacher and she allowed me to turn the thing for extra credit. I still don't know how that ended up working, but it did. I managed to turn the thing into a trilogy before I graduated high school.

Now, in 2018 I hope to see my writing career go further than I ever thought possible, and with time I know this will just be the first steps into something truly amazing.

To learn more about Jesse Wilson and discover more Next Chapter authors, visit our website at www.nextchapter.pub.

Flesh and Iron
ISBN: 978-4-82419-745-0

Published by
Next Chapter
2-5-6 SANNO
SANNO BRIDGE
143-0023 Ota-Ku, Tokyo
+818035793528

3rd September 2024

Milton Keynes UK
Ingram Content Group UK Ltd.
UKHW041818151124
451262UK00005B/659